Danger in Dinosaur Valley

Roy MacGregor

An M&S Paperback Original from
McClelland & Stewart Ltd.
The Canadian Publishers

PS 8575 .G84 D36 1999 cuppi...

For Shauna, Logan and Hope Kearns

The author is grateful to Doug Gibson, who thought up this
series, and to Alex Schultz, who pulls it off.

National Library of Canada Cataloguing in Publication Data

MacGregor, Roy, 1948–
    Danger in Dinosaur Valley

(The Screech Owls series; 10)
"An M&S paperback original."
ISBN 0-7710-5620-6

I. Title. II. Series: MacGregor, Roy, 1948– .
The Screech Owls series.

PS8575.G84D36 1999   jC813'.54   C98-932852-x
PZ7.M33D3 1999

We acknowledge the financial support of the Government of
Canada through the Book Publishing Industry Development
Program for our publishing activities. We further acknowledge
the support given by the Canada Council for the Arts for our
publishing program.

Cover illustration by Gregory C. Banning
Typeset in Bembo by M&S, Toronto

Printed and bound in Canada

McClelland & Stewart Ltd.
The Canadian Publishers
481 University Avenue
Toronto, Ontario
M5G 2E9
www.mcclelland.com

3 4 5 6 7   06 05 04 03 02

"PLEASE STATE YOUR NAME."

Travis Lindsay had never shaken so much in his life. Not from the cold wind of James Bay. Not from the thrill of Disney World's Tower of Terror. Not even from the emotion of seeing Data wheeled out onto the ice the night of the benefit game.

This was different: this was pure nerves.

Travis was terrified.

He was not so much frightened of a lie – which was why he was here – but petrified, to the very bottom of his twelve-year-old soul, of the *truth*.

"Your name?"

The man asking the question was staring at Travis, waiting. He was an older man – an officer of the Royal Canadian Mounted Police – with a white brush cut so thick and stiff it looked as if he could sand wood with the top of his head. His face, however, was soft and flushed. He had his uniform jacket off, and there were sweat stains under the arms of his shirt. A second Mountie, younger, square-jawed and unsmiling, sat closer to the window, where he was surrounded by computer equipment and switches. An open Pepsi can was on the desk in front of him, condensation beading on the sides. Travis was suddenly aware of how badly he himself wanted something cold to drink.

Travis cleared his throat to answer. A green line on the computer screen jumped. The Mountie monitoring the line checked off something on a pad.

"T—Travis Lindsay," he finally said, his voice catching.

Even in the heat of the small room, he could feel the shiver of cold metal on his skin. There were electrodes taped over his heart and to his arm, and sensors attached to his temples and even to the index finger of his right hand. He tried to tell his body parts not to jump — but they seemed to belong to someone else.

"Address?"

"Twenty-two Birch Street, Tamarack." He tried to be helpful: "You want my postal code?"

The Mountie asking the questions shook his head. The other Mountie looked up at him, blinking, and again checked something off on the pad. *Did he think Travis was trying to be smart?*

"This is just to set the parameters of the computer," the first Mountie said. "Just relax, son."

Relax? Easy for him to say. He wasn't the one

on trial here, in the middle of the strangest land any of the Screech Owls had ever visited.

How could Travis possibly relax when he'd just seen his best friend, Wayne Nishikawa, leave this same room in the Drumheller RCMP headquarters with tears streaming down his red cheeks? How could he relax when so many of his teammates were waiting in another room to go through the same gruelling experience. Sarah was out there. And Lars. And Jenny. And Jesse. And Andy. Each one of them waiting to take a lie-detector test.

It seemed the whole world had been turned upside down. It was March break, and yet the younger Mountie had just pried open the window, and the welcome breeze that fluttered the paper on the desks felt like summer. Over the hum of the computer, Travis could hear the river churning behind the curling rink across the street. Between the Owls' departure from Tamarack and this dreadful moment, winter had vanished like one of those time-lapse shots the nature shows sometimes had of flowers opening in super-fast motion. One day winter snowploughs in the streets, the next day flooding along the low riverbanks.

There were television cameras in town – somehow, word had got out – though this was no nature program. This was closer to science fiction, but there was no button on a remote to push so that the two Mounted Police would simply flash into a shrinking dot of light on a dark screen. This was real life – *only it couldn't possibly be! Could it?*

"All right, Travis," the first Mountie said, apparently satisfied with the levels he was getting off the monitors, "I'm going to ask you a series of questions, now. You're simply to answer them honestly, understand?"

Travis cleared his throat again. The green readout line jumped sharply.

"Yes, sir."

The Mountie asking the questions smiled gently, then began.

"You are a member of a hockey team, correct?"

"Yes."

"The name of the team?"

"The Screech Owls."

"And you're out here for a tournament, isn't that right?"

"Yes."

"The name of the tournament?"

Travis's mind wasn't working right. He couldn't remember. The Prairie Invitational? The Drumheller Invitational? The Alberta Invitational? Was the word "peewee" in there anywhere? He didn't want the two Mounties to think him so stupid, so he tried to bluff his way through the question.

"Prairie Invitational . . . ?" he answered hesitantly.

The green readout light jumped, a squiggly line like a ragged mountain range forming on the screen. The two Mounties looked at each other.

The first Mountie smiled. "Care to try again, Travis?"

Travis coughed. The line jumped. "I, I don't remember exactly," Travis said. "*Something* Invitational. I'm sorry."

"Drumheller Invitational Peewee Tournament," the first Mountie said, smiling as he scribbled something in his notes.

The man didn't appear at all bothered by Travis's error. In fact, he looked oddly pleased, as if Travis's little mistake had confirmed something. Travis didn't know if that was good or bad, but it seemed the lie detector would react whenever he wasn't absolutely certain of his answer. He would do no more guessing. And he would certainly not be lying – whether he was hooked up to a lie detector or not.

"What happened yesterday to you and your teammates, Travis?"

Travis sucked his breath in deep. He felt like he was going to explode. In trying so hard to appear calm, he was only making it worse. His arms and legs were jumping on their own. His throat felt dry and tight. But there was no choice but to begin, and to let the machine do its job. It was all so incredible to Travis. He was no longer sure himself what had happened – and what he had seen.

"We, we went out on the bikes . . ."

"Where?"

"Out along the river. We wanted to look for hoodoos."

The Mountie nodded, one eye seemingly on Travis, the other tracking the readout line of the computer. The line was a little wiggly, but steady, with neither high jagged mountains nor sharp valleys.

"And?"

"And we also wanted to see where Nish had been."

"Who's Nish?"

"Wayne Nishikawa. We call him Nish."

"Your friend."

"Yes."

"Nish had already been there?"

"Yes."

"And what made this place so interesting?"

"It was where he saw . . . the . . ." Travis's throat went thin as a straw. He could barely breathe, let alone speak.

Both Mounties looked up, waiting.

"Where he saw the what, Travis?" the first Mountie asked.

"The . . . the *thing* he saw."

6

"The *thing* he saw?" the Mountie repeated. Travis thought he could detect a little sarcasm there. Clearly, they didn't think Nish had seen anything at all.

"Yes."

"Did you believe Nish had seen anything?"

"No," Travis said. "Not then, anyway."

The Mounties exchanged the quickest of glances. Travis noticed that the second Mountie, the one handling the computer, was smiling slightly. Travis didn't like the look of that smile.

"And did you find the right place?"

"We rode off the trail and back over some hills," Travis said. "I'm not sure exactly where we were . . ."

"Did you see anything?"

Travis looked down, swallowing hard.

"Yes." He spoke almost defiantly, certain that he would be challenged.

"And what did you see, Travis?"

Travis moved his lips but nothing came out. He tried to breathe in, but his lungs had frozen. He felt slightly dizzy and shifted in his seat. He wanted to scream. No wonder Nish had run out of the room crying. Travis felt close to tears himself.

"What was it you saw?" the first Mountie asked again.

"I, I'm not *sure* . . ." Travis said.

Both men looked at him hard.

7

"Do you mean you might have seen *nothing*?" the first Mountie asked.

"No."

The Mountie's red face darkened further.

"But you're not *sure* what you saw?" he asked, his lips narrowing.

"No, not that. I know what I saw. But I can't *believe* what I saw."

The first Mountie smiled, encouraging.

"Just say what you think you saw, then."

Travis sat up in his seat, blowing air hard out of his cheeks. He swallowed and looked directly into the Mountie's eyes.

"A dinosaur."

Travis looked from one Mountie to the other, waiting for a reaction. The first Mountie was staring down at his monitor, watching the thin green line. The second was also staring at a monitor.

The first Mountie expelled a burst of air just as Travis had done moments earlier. The colour had drained completely from his face. He looked ashen.

Travis knew why. He felt queasy himself.

The line hadn't even flickered!

2

WHERE TO BEGIN? TRAVIS WONDERED. HE HAD already telephoned home to talk to his mother and father, and even though they'd been sympathetic and supportive, Travis couldn't shake the feeling that they didn't believe him either. And who could blame them? If his best friend Nish had come up with this story, Travis would have aimed his index finger at his right temple and spun it around and around and around. It was absolutely *insane*.

The Screech Owls hockey team had flown to Calgary, Alberta, on a sparkling-clear and bitterly cold March day. They had stuffed their thick winter coats into the overhead containers and settled down with their books and portable CD players and hockey magazines for what was sure to be one of the greatest Screech Owls escapades of all time.

They were headed for the town of Drumheller, where the Owls were going to combine a hockey tournament with a tour of the famous Badlands and a visit to the world-famous Royal Tyrrell Museum. At the Royal Tyrrell, they were going to learn all about prehistoric life in North America. They were headed, claimed Data, who always seemed to know about such things, to "The Dinosaur Capital of Canada."

They would be seeing prehistoric fossils and models of the giant reptiles that had lived in the Badlands nearly a hundred million years ago – a time so far in the past that Travis and the rest of the Owls couldn't even comprehend its distance. Data said to think of it this way: at twelve years of age, they had each been alive 4,380 days, or 105,120 hours, or 6,307,200 minutes. If every minute of their lives had really taken twenty years to live, that's how long ago the dinosaurs lived in Alberta.

"Every minute *does* last twenty years!" Nish had roared. "At least when you're in Mr. Schultz's math class!"

The Owls were so excited about the trip they had all but forgotten about the hockey. Muck Munro hadn't been able to get off work and so they were without a coach. One of the assistants, Ty Barrett, had managed to get time off, but Ty wasn't that much older than the Owls themselves. Control of the team had pretty much fallen to Mr. Higgins, Andy's father, and good old Mr. Dillinger, who had actually taken an extra week off work so he could drive the Screech Owls' bus to Calgary, meet them there, and then drive them around Drumheller and the surrounding area while the tournament was on. Once it was over,

Mr. Dillinger was going to drive all the way back home while everyone else flew.

They could never have afforded the trip if Mr. Higgins hadn't become involved. Before Andy's family had moved to Ontario so Mr. Higgins could supervise a huge gas-pipeline project, he had been an executive with one of the biggest oil companies in Alberta. Through years of travel, he had built up enough air-travel points, Andy once said, to fly the family five times around the world. When Mr. Higgins then won a special airline draw that gave him a million bonus points on his air-travel program, he had generously donated all his points to the Owls. The entire team was able to fly out and back – at no cost at all to the players!

Once Mr. Higgins got involved, there was no holding him back. A big man with a salesman's gift for persuasion, he had easily talked Mr. Dillinger into taking the old bus across country so the Owls would have cheap transportation once they got to Calgary. He also arranged accommodation on the outskirts of Drumheller where an old friend of his, Kelly Block, had a sports camp that specialized in motivation and teamwork. They might not win the hockey tournament, Mr. Higgins had said at a meeting of all the players and their parents, but they'd come back a better team!

Most of the parents had seemed quite pleased with the arrangement, and were even excited about the idea of a motivational sports camp.

Travis had noticed, however, that Muck, who had earlier said he might not even come to the meeting, slipped out of the hall before it was over. From his seat by the window, Travis could see Muck walking in the freezing parking lot, his breath lingering in heavy clouds as he moved slowly back and forth on his bad leg. He knew Muck well enough to know that the coach was unhappy about something.

Now that they had arrived, Travis thought he knew what had disturbed his old coach. Following supper that first night in Drumheller, he had overheard Mr. Higgins and Kelly Block talking, and he hadn't liked the tone Kelly Block was using. The camp owner – an athletic-looking man with his blond hair strangely combed over the bald spots – seemed to be dumping on Muck, whom he didn't even know, for being old-fashioned and out of touch with modern coaching techniques. At one point Block had even said it was "time for the Screech Owls to move on, get a new coach who understands the way the game is played today." Travis had felt his cheeks burn with anger. Already he didn't like Kelly Block.

"*Mental* Block" was the nickname Nish had already given the head of the sports camp, and it seemed to be sticking – at least when the Owls talked to each other in private.

Travis had tried to imagine the trip west for

weeks, but his daydreams had fallen very far short of reality. Three hours into their flight, they had flown straight into a chinook that had blown up across the Rocky Mountains from the United States. The plane had bounced into the rush of warm air from the south like a fishing bobber in a rough current. Poor Nish barely had time to scream "I'M GONNA HURL!" before he turned pure white and was reaching for a barf bag.

They landed in summer weather – an entire hockey team wearing three layers of clothing, including long underwear, and carrying their bulky Screech Owls parkas, scarves, tuques, and heavy winter mitts. It was as if they'd flown to Florida, not Calgary. The heat made them itchy and cranky. Mr. Dillinger, who was there to meet them, was having trouble with the bus overheating and twice had to stop to let the engine cool down while the Owls filed out along the shoulder of the road in their shirtsleeves and marvelled at the extraordinarily warm wind.

"It's a chinook," Andy said.

"We get sudden thaws back home in Tamarack sometimes," said Fahd.

Andy shook his head sharply. "Not the same thing. You only get chinooks out here. I've seen them last for more than a week."

They drove with the windows open, the tired travellers dozing, the road straight as a ruler, the landscape flat for the most part and sometimes rolling slightly. There were small lakes in the fields from the quickly melting snow.

They were passing through a small town – Beiseker, the sign said – when, up ahead in the bus, Sarah suddenly broke into wild laughter.

"*We're in Nish's home town! They even put up a statue to him!*"

Everyone sat up and looked outside. They were passing a baseball diamond, and then a park, and in the middle of the park was a large black-and-white statue of – *a skunk!*

The big statue even had a sign with the skunk's name: SQUIRT.

Nish stood in the aisle, turning as he bowed in acceptance. "Thank you very much, thank you very much."

Soon, however, the joking died down. Several of the Owls were asleep. Travis put his jacket against the window and leaned against it, one eye barely watching the rolling fields and the telephone poles pass by.

The next thing Travis knew, he was being jarred awake by a wildly honking horn. Travis sat up sharply, his chin on the seat in front. All the other Owls were also popping up wide awake. At the front, Mr. Dillinger's bald head was turning rapidly back and forth as he leaned on the horn and tried to see if everyone was up and watching. He was laughing and excited.

"*Get ready to drop off the edge of the Earth!*" Mr.

Dillinger shouted, giggling at the end of his warning.

"THE ROAD'S WASHED OUT!" Nish screamed from the back of the bus.

Travis stared ahead through the patch in the windshield where the wipers had cleared the muddy spray from passing vehicles. To either side he could still see the wet brown fields of the flat Alberta countryside, but up ahead the ground – and the road they were following – had vanished!

"HERE WE GO!" shouted Mr. Dillinger. "HANG ONTO YOUR HATS!"

Travis could not even get his breath. The bus rumbled on, Mr. Dillinger seemingly unconcerned that up ahead there was no road whatsoever, just open space and fog!

"WE'RE GONNA DIE!" Nish shouted. "WE'RE ALL GONNA DIE!"

The bus hurtled towards the edge, then *dropped*. Not like a stone, but like a glider, sailing down into thick fog.

Travis felt his ears pop as the bus seemed to float, down, down, down the steep slope of the highway into the fog.

It really did seem they had dropped off the edge of the Earth, just as the old explorers were warned would happen if they dared set out to sail *around* a world that everyone knew was flat as a board.

"WE'RE GONNA DIE!"

Travis didn't have to see Nish's face, or anyone else's for that matter, to know that they were as delighted as he was by the thrilling ride. This was an added bonus.

A hockey tournament.

A visit to a fabulous dinosaur museum.

And a brand-new world to explore.

This was going to be an unbelievable Screech Owls adventure.

3

"*'QUESTION 3: WOULD YOU RATHER PASS WIND or make a speech?'*" Nish read out loud from his dressing-room locker. "WHAT IS THIS?"

"Aren't they pretty well the same thing for you?" Sarah asked from a stall on the other side.

The Owls all had their heads down, trying to fill in the blanks on a document they were balancing on the tops of their shin pads and hockey pants. They had just had their first practice at the Drumheller arena – a marvellous rink, where the Zamboni drove onto the ice through the mouth of a dinosaur and green dinosaurs were painted into each side of the faceoff circle – and then Kelly Block had handed out an eight-page questionnaire that he said would help him get to know the team. He wanted what he called "psychological profiles" of the whole team.

Travis understood some of the questions – "*Do you feel you have leadership qualities? . . . If you play well but the team still loses, are you satisfied?*" – but a good many of them made no sense whatsoever. The Owls were asked about their ambitions and interests, as might be expected, but also about daydreaming and private fears and, as Nish had just loudly pointed out, even passing wind.

"GIVE ME A BREAK!" Nish shouted from the corner. "'*Question 14: Would you rather kiss a member of the opposite sex or finish your homework?*'"

"I picked homework," Sarah said.

"I'd rather pick my nose," grumbled Nish, burying his head in the final page of the questionnaire.

Kelly Block came in and rounded up the finished questionnaires. He had that slightly knock-kneed, bounce-on-the-balls-of-the-feet way of moving. He was wearing expensive running shoes without the laces tied up, and he had on a track suit with his name stencilled over the heart and the name of his business – Camp Victory – emblazoned across the back.

Camp Victory must have been mostly a summer operation, for it had a musty smell to it that suggested the place had only recently been opened up and still needed some airing out. Fortunately, it was like summer right now. If it had been typical March weather, and the windows had remained locked up tight, the camp buildings might have been unbearable. Travis figured Kelly Block spent most of the winter months working for big companies like the one Mr. Higgins was with. Judging from Block's clothes and the expensive 4x4 sports utility vehicle he drove, Travis figured he must do pretty well as a motivational psychologist.

Certainly, he had spent a lot of money setting up this camp. There was a main building with a full gymnasium – weights, workout bikes, treadmills – and a kitchen that served meals so good that Nish forgot he'd seen the golden arches of McDonald's on the drive into town. There were individual cabins, each with four beds and the hottest, softest showers Travis had ever been under. There was a small enclosed rink for Rollerblade hockey, a basketball court, and a "garage" filled with mountain bikes, good ones with full shocks.

The Drumheller area was a mountain-biker's dream, with deep valleys and high rounded hills and natural trails everywhere you looked. The camp was out along the Red Deer River, halfway to a suspension footbridge at Rosedale that headed deep into the hills. They had already been out past Rosedale to see the hoodoos – bizarre, cartoon-like pillars of rock the shape of mushrooms and monsters that had been formed by thousands of years of erosion – and there were said to be more hoodoos farther up a trail beyond the swinging bridge. It was more like they'd come to another planet than another town.

"We did die when the bus went over that hill," Nish announced. "And this is heaven!"

"Not if *you're* here, it isn't," corrected Sarah.

In Mr. Dillinger's old team bus, they had toured the town and the surrounding countryside. Drumheller was fascinating, with dinosaur models – some of them life-size – at every corner, and dinosaur murals painted on most of the buildings. They visited the Little Church, a building so tiny they had to take turns just to get inside and see. "SEATS 10,000," a sign said. "SIX AT A TIME."

"How come they don't have a little priest?" Nish asked aloud when the others were trying to sit and kneel in their seats. "And a little Bible and a little God and a little Jesus?"

"How about a little *quiet*?" Sarah said over her shoulder.

They stopped for the better part of the afternoon at the fabulous Royal Tyrrell Museum of Paleontology, a huge complex on the other side of town, deep in the high, barren hills. Travis had seen dozens of museums in his lifetime, but never one so spectacular as this. It sat, like a spaceship on the moon, perfectly placed in what seemed its very own canyon.

Outside were bronzed, full-sized models of various dinosaurs. Travis thought if the museum weren't there, someone who happened to walk in here over the hills could easily think they had stepped back in time a hundred million years. It sent a shudder of excitement up his spine.

Mr. Higgins had arranged for a special tour of the museum. Mr. Dillinger got Data's wheelchair out of the bus, and Sarah was quick to move in behind it to push him around. The Owls set off, and were soon swarming around displays of huge jawbones and skulls of dozens of prehistoric beasts, including one magnificent model of what looked like a giant flesh-eating Tyrannosaurus rex. The monster was fighting a couple of small, vicious Domeosaurs over the bloody remains of a dead Parasaurolophus.

"Sick," said Jenny.

"Awesome," said Fahd.

"It's not a Tyrannosaurus," corrected Data. "It's an Albertosaurus."

"Good for you," smiled the guide. "A much tougher beast than T. rex. How did you know that?"

"I study dinosaurs," Data said, blushing.

"I want to see an Ontariosaurus!" called Nish.

"Sorry," said the guide. "There's no such thing."

"That's not true," Sarah whispered to the rest of the Owls. "There's Nish. He's creepy. He's got a brain the size of a peanut. He makes your skin crawl. And he's from Ontario."

Nish turned sharply as the others began giggling. "*What's so funny?*" he demanded. But no one would tell him.

Travis had never had such a marvellous day. The Owls were taken on a hike around the neighbouring hills, and were shown where fossils had been dug out of the ground. They were told that alligators had once lived here. They were told that there were still dangerous beasts about, not dinosaurs but poisonous snakes and scorpions and black widow spiders, and that they had better be careful where they stepped.

The Owls visited a lab and saw scientists cleaning newly discovered fossils and getting ready to assemble the skeletons. They saw fossils embedded in rocks, and whole reconstructed skeletons, and artists' depictions of life, and death, as it must have been more than a hundred million years ago. They learned that dinosaurs might have lived to be as much as 150 years old. They learned that no one really knows what the largest dinosaurs were, though the Brachiosaurus stood as tall as a five-storey building and weighed as much eighty tonnes. They learned that the smallest dinosaur was no bigger than a chicken, and that the toughest dinosaur was not, as they had thought, Tyrannosaurus rex. The most fearsome of all was a little featherweight called Deinonychus, which was no bigger than a man but could move so fast and slash so quickly with its long, sickle-shaped claws and razor-sharp teeth that no dinosaur would dare tangle with it. They learned that they were standing on the richest dinosaur land known on Earth: some thirty-five different dinosaur species had been identified in the Alberta Badlands.

"There's so much we don't know," said the guide. "Before 1824 they didn't even know dinosaurs once existed. We don't know whether they were cold- or warm-blooded. We don't know what colour they were. We don't even know what they sounded like."

"Did they fart?" a small voice squeaked from the back.

"Excuse me?" the guide said, trying to see who had spoken.

No one spoke. Travis cringed, knowing at once who it was.

"You said something, young man?" the guide said pointedly to Nish.

"N—no," Nish mumbled.

"I didn't think so," the guide said. "If you have something to say, please tell us all, though, will you?"

"O . . . kay," Nish mumbled even lower.

"Ontariosaurus," Sarah said. Everyone, the guide included, laughed.

"Actually, young man, we do have something over here you might be interested in."

They crossed to a special display, and the guide stopped in front of what appeared to be a polished rock.

"Any idea what this might be, young man?" the guide asked Nish.

Nish looked, his eyes squinting with suspicion. "N—no."

"It's *coprolites*. Anyone have any idea what that means?"

The guide looked around. Data was raising his hand.

"Yes?" the guide asked.

"It's dung, isn't it?"

The guide's eyes lighted up. "Good for you. Yes, dung. Prehistoric poop. This one's probably twenty million years old."

"Does it still smell?" Nish asked.

"A smell wouldn't last twenty million years, young man," the guide said, shaking his head.

"You obviously haven't spent much time around Nish," Wilson said, breaking up the group.

"*Very funny*," Nish snapped, and stormed off.

It wasn't a good day for Nish at the Royal Tyrrell Museum — but that was nothing compared to the evening he had back at Camp Victory. After a good meal, the Owls had been sitting around, talking about their wonderful day at the dinosaur museum, when Kelly Block walked in and announced that their day wasn't done yet.

"We are going to build a team," Block announced.

"We already are a team," Nish protested, but he wilted under the stern gaze of Kelly Block.

"You are, are you?" Block asked, his eyebrows rising.

"We're the Screech Owls," Nish said weakly.

"Your name?"

"Wayne," Nish said.

"Nish," Fahd corrected.

Block smiled. "So, Mr. Nish, do you know what makes a team?"

Nish had turned crimson. "I guess. . . . Kids who play together. A coach."

Block laughed. It was an ugly laugh. It seemed fake to Travis, and it had an insulting tone to it. "Not even close, mister."

Block, who had been sitting cross-legged on the floor as he talked to them, suddenly sprang to his feet. He stood himself in front of Nish.

"Stand up," he instructed.

Nish reluctantly got to his feet. Travis could see that he was sweating.

Block pulled a chair out from a table and set it in the middle of the floor.

"Stand up here," Block commanded.

Slowly, Nish climbed up onto the chair and stood.

Kelly Block pulled a handkerchief from his jacket pocket. "Lean towards me," he commanded. Nish leaned forward and Block tied the handkerchief over his eyes. He then straightened Nish up, keeping one hand on Nish's arm to keep him from falling.

"You," he said, pointing towards Sarah. "Back there." He pointed behind Nish.

Travis realized at that moment that Kelly Block was no fool. He had already understood that there was a rivalry between Nish and Sarah.

Sarah rose, smiling, and stood where she was told behind Nish.

Block stared up at Nish.

"I'm going to push you over backwards," he said. "One of your teammates will catch you. Do you understand?"

"N–no," Nish said. His voice shook.

"I assure you that one of your teammates is behind you and will stop your fall," Block said. "Do you believe me?"

"I–I guess so."

"You don't sound very certain."

"I can't see anyone."

"But it's your teammate. Wouldn't they automatically be there to save you?"

"I don't know."

"You don't know," Block said with sarcasm. "You don't know. What kind of 'team' is that, where you don't know your own teammates?"

"I don't know." Nish repeated. He sounded near tears.

"I'm going to push you back," Block warned. "Are you ready?"

Nish was breathing hard. "N–no."

"Your teammate is there, waiting to catch you."

26

He turned to Sarah. "Are you ready to catch him?"

"Yes."

Travis could see Nish jump with the realization that it was Sarah waiting behind him. Sarah, who never let Nish get away with anything. Sarah, who knew exactly how to wind Nish up or shut Nish down, whatever the situation required.

"Here goes," Kelly Block said.

He placed a large hand over Nish's chest, and pushed back. Sarah prepared to catch him.

Nish buckled! He folded and toppled forward rather than back, falling into Kelly Block's big hands instead of back onto Sarah.

Block caught Nish easily and ripped off the handkerchief.

Travis noted Block's smile. He had expected this.

Travis could see the terror in Nish's eyes. And humiliation. And anger. He had been singled out, he had been tested, and he had failed. Nish wouldn't look at Sarah, who also looked hurt. She had wanted to catch Nish. Travis knew she would never have let Nish fall and hurt himself.

But Kelly Block was ignoring both of them. He was standing in the centre of the room, bouncing on the balls of his feet, his hands out in front of him as if he were holding a phantom football. He nodded his head knowingly.

"There is no team here," he announced. "We have a lot of work to do."

4

THERE WAS NO TIME, HOWEVER, FOR KELLY Block to do anything about the Screech Owls' team spirit before they played their first game. The Drumheller Invitational Peewee Tournament was getting under way first thing the next morning, with the Owls scheduled to play their first match against the Hanna Hurricanes.

"That's Lanny McDonald's home town!" Data had shouted as Mr. Dillinger read out the schedule to the Owls gathered in the dressing room.

"Maybe they've all got big red moustaches!" Nish shouted.

Travis giggled, thinking of a bunch of twelve-year-old boys and girls skating out looking like they were Yosemite Sam from the Saturday-afternoon cartoon shows. He was a great fan of Lanny McDonald, even if he'd never seen the Hall of Famer play in the NHL. He knew that Lanny had scored a big goal for the Calgary Flames the year they won the Stanley Cup, and he knew, of course, that Lanny McDonald not only played with heart, he approached life the same way. He'd come all the way to Tamarack, after all, for the big fundraiser after Data was hurt by the car.

It was time for the Screech Owls to hit the ice.

"LET'S GO!" Sarah called, slamming her stick hard onto the concrete floor of the dressing room. Travis, the captain, hadn't even put his helmet on yet! He scrambled to catch up, joining in the shouting.

"C'MON SARAH – A COUPLE OF GOALS!"

"MAKE YOUR FIRST SHOT COUNT, DMITRI!"

"BE TOUGH, LARS! BE STRONG!"

"MOVE YOUR BIG BUTT, NISH!"

Travis moved quickly through the door leading to the ice surface, Data slapping the rear of his pants as he passed. Travis had come to count on Data's slap as much as he needed to hit the crossbar in warmup. Data being there meant a lot to the Owls – he had, in some ways, become as important a coach as Muck himself. Not for how he planned out the games and changed the lines, but for how his own intensity and desire seemed to rub off on the others.

Travis stepped out onto the ice of the little arena knowing there was nothing he'd rather be doing. It might have been like summer outside, but in here the air was cool and the ice as hard as glass. He could hear his skates dig in on the corners. He could hear the buzz of the crowd. It seemed as if the entire town of Hanna had driven down for the game. Travis hit the crossbar on his first shot, a high snapper over Jenny's left shoulder. He slammed his stick triumphantly into the boards as he swooped past the net and turned back towards the blueline.

The crossbar was a good omen. Sarah took the opening faceoff and turned her back on her checker, giving her time to send the puck back to Nish, who was already in motion. Nish crossed his own blueline and – just as his skates touched the tail of the green dinosaur on the Owls' side of centre – sent a high, looping pass up the right side for Dmitri, who timed it perfectly, snaring the puck just as it crossed the Hurricanes' blueline. There were cries in the crowd that Dmitri was offside, but Travis knew better. Dmitri's astonishing speed often made him look offside, and besides, the linesman had been right there as he crossed.

The Hurricanes' defence was quick, however, and Dmitri's route to the net was cut off. But for Dmitri it was no problem: he did his reverse curl, heading directly towards the boards, and then cutting back up towards the blueline. The move worked beautifully. As he headed in one direction, everyone else went the other way. He caught Sarah perfectly as she slipped over the blueline. Sarah dished a backhand pass to Travis, cutting in from his wing, and then took out her defender. Travis found he was all alone, one-on-one with the Hanna goaltender. A quick deke to the backhand and Travis lifted the puck high as he could as he flew past the net, the goaltender sprawling. He couldn't see what happened, but the *ping* off the crossbar followed by the whistle told him he had scored – and it was a beauty!

Screech Owls 1, Hurricanes 0.

One shift and they were already ahead. A grateful Mr. Dillinger was all over Travis's line, tossing towels over the necks of Travis, Sarah, and Dmitri as they skated off and took the bench. *Towels* – and they hadn't even broken a sweat! Data wheeled along the cramped space behind the bench and slapped each of them on the back.

Travis turned to high-five Data – and then saw that the Screech Owls had another coach. Kelly Block! He was standing beside Ty, seeming to dwarf the young assistant coach.

"*What's 'Mental Block' doin' here?*" Nish hissed in Travis's ear.

Travis shrugged. "I don't know. I guess he just appointed himself coach."

"If Muck was here he'd toss him out of the rink."

Travis shrugged again. He didn't know. If Muck were here, he doubted Block, for all his nerve, would have the guts to step in beside the Owls' coach. But Muck wasn't here, and Block was trampling over poor Mr. Dillinger right in front of their eyes – or, more accurately, right behind their backs.

Travis felt Kelly Block's hands on his neck, rubbing hard through the towel. He didn't like the feeling at all.

"*Atta boy, Trav! Way to go out there! You just keep open for Sarah to hit you – you got it?*"

Got it? Travis wondered. *What's this guy talking about?* Of course he'd try to get open for Sarah. They'd been playing together so long now, neither of them, or Dmitri, for that matter, even had to think about what the play might be. It was as if three players – Travis, Sarah, and Dmitri – shared one mind. But here was this smarmy "sports psychologist" acting as if he'd come up with the play himself.

Soon, Andy had scored a lovely goal on a hard slapshot through traffic. Fahd scored – a bit of a surprise – on a play in which he seemed to walk in, in slow motion, from the blueline and slip the puck under the arm of the falling Hurricanes goaltender. Jesse Highboy scored on a tip-in, and Wilson scored on a weak backhander that went in off a defenceman's skate.

Screech Owls 5, Hurricanes 0.

It was clear by the end of the first period that the team from Hanna was badly outclassed by the Owls. Instinctively, the Owls began to hold back a bit, knowing that Muck never, ever wanted them to run up the score on a team. "Never humiliate an opponent," he used to say. "You try to embarrass the team you're playing against, you really just embarrass yourself."

Kelly Block, however, began to take over at the break. While Mr. Dillinger hung his head low and stayed in the background, working on Sarah's skates, Block tried to make a speech that only caused Nish to get the giggles. He talked about how these tournaments are often decided on goals as well as points, and how the Owls had better make every shot count. Kelly Block's eyes, Travis noticed, had taken on a new look. It was as if they were on fire. Travis found he couldn't look him straight in the eye.

By the middle of the second period, Block had taken over completely. He was calling the line changes. He was standing directly behind the players, rocking on the balls of his feet and chewing on ice the way some of the big-league coaches did. He was ignoring Mr. Dillinger and Ty and even Data.

Travis felt the hand on his neck again.

"Trav," Kelly Block's voice growled into his ear, "I'm going to shake up the lines a bit, okay?"

Travis didn't know what to say. *Shake up what lines? And why?* But he knew what he was expected to say, and he said it: "Okay."

"Sarah!" Kelly Block shouted. "Out with Jesse Highboy – and you, Liz!"

Up and down the bench heads bobbed up, helmets turning back and forth as friends and teammates tried to catch each other's eye. *What was going on here?*

Travis noticed that Kelly Block had a list in his pocket that he kept referring to and making changes on with a pen. It was crazy. Sarah had never played with Jesse or Liz in her life. And who did Block want *him* to play with?

"*Nishikawa!*" Block shouted after an offside whistle. "You're centring Travis and Andy!"

Instinctively, Travis turned to see if Nish would look in his direction, and sure enough, his best friend shot him a glance. Nish looked as if they'd just stepped into an insane asylum and some nut had taken charge of the Owls. *Nish at centre?* Not likely.

Sarah's expression said pretty much the same thing: *Who is this guy? What is going on here? Where's Muck?*

Nish didn't even know how to line up for the faceoff. Twice, the linesman had to correct his stance. Then he threw Nish out of the circle. Red-faced and angry, Nish had to let Travis take over the draw.

Travis won the faceoff and sent it back to the defence – but the defence turned out to be Derek Dillinger! Derek, who'd never played defence before, lost the puck in his skates and let it slip away into open ice, where a quick little Hurricanes forward picked it up and flew down on Jeremy, scoring high to the stick side.

When they got back to the bench Kelly Block was furious. He benched Derek for losing the puck and Nish for getting thrown out of the faceoff circle.

"You had nothing to do with it," Travis told his friend, hoping to comfort him.

"He hates my guts," Nish said. "That's all that's going on here. He hates me."

"Maybe he knows what he's doing," Travis said. "He's a sports psychologist after all."

"Yeah, right – and I'm a rocket scientist."

By the third period, Kelly Block was setting lines as if he were drawing names from a hat. The confusion was so enormous, he obviously felt he had to explain himself.

"This is a great opportunity for us to try out some new combinations," he said during a quiet break in the play. "We've got a lot of work to do on team chemistry."

Travis could only shake his head. "Team chemistry" never used to be a problem. Muck hadn't put the Owls together as if he'd dropped a pack of cards and simply picked it up in whatever order he found it. The Owls had been years in the making. Most of them went all the way back to mite together. Travis and Sarah had first played together in novice. And as long as they'd been peewee players, they had played with Dmitri on the first line. The top line.

Now there was no top line. No lines at all, it seemed. Defencemen were playing up, forwards back. Travis wondered if Block would yank Jeremy out of goal in the final few minutes and put him at centre.

The Hurricanes used the confusion to edge their way bit by bit back into the game. They brought the score to 5–3 with two minutes to go, when Sarah, now back on defence, began an end-to-end rush that left a soft rebound lying at the edge of the crease, and Dmitri backhanded it home so high and hard the goaltender's water bottle flew through the air and shot its contents all over the glass in front of the goal judge.

"*Atta girl, Sarah!*" Kelly Block shouted as they returned to the bench. "You're a natural defence-man – sorry, defence-*person*!"

Sarah said nothing. Travis had never seen his friend so unhappy about setting up a goal.

But Sarah's discomfort was nothing compared to Nish's. Nish was sitting at the far end of the bench, pounding his skates into the board to keep the circulation flowing in his feet. Travis could tell, even at that distance, that he was crying. But he wasn't sure why.

Frozen feet?

Or frozen out?

5

IN THE MORNING, KELLY BLOCK IMMEDIATELY
began to work on building "team chemistry." He
had the Screech Owls take turns standing on the
chair and falling backwards; they knew that when
they fell, someone – a teammate – would be there
to catch them. Even Nish managed to shut his
eyes and fall back, first into Andy's arms and then
Simon's, once he'd seen Sarah and Travis and Lars
and Dmitri and Derek and Liz do the same without so much as a nervous tremor.

Travis was beginning to understand what Block
was up to. When the sports psychologist talked
about a team being like a chain, and "only as strong
as its weakest link," Travis could see how that made
sense on a hockey team. It was fine to have puck-
carriers and goal-scorers, but unless there was a
solid defence to back them up, the game would
become more like basketball – last shot wins. And
it was fine to have forwards who were good in front
of the net, but unless there were forwards who
were also good in the corners, the puck was never
going to get to the front of the net. And as for the
goalie, well, that was the most important position

of all, wasn't it? Travis didn't think there was a position in all of sports – not baseball pitcher, not even football quarterback – that had as much pressure as goaltender. Pitchers didn't have to play every game, or even every second game. And there was no coach on the sidelines to send in plays to a goaltender the way they did in football.

To reinforce his "link" theory, and to get the Owls depending on each other off the ice as well as on, Block had a few more exercises for them to try. The best involved a nearby creek that emptied into the Red Deer River, a creek that was now swollen with the runoff from the recently snow-covered hills. Block had them build a "bridge" to get across it. He put half the team on one side of the creek, and half the team on the other. They had to assemble a platform on each side using logs and boards, fitting and clamping them together without the aid of plans. Then they had to figure out how to get a cable across from one platform to the other so that one of the Owls could cross the creek. They tried throwing the cable across, but the creek was too wide and the line fell short. On Nish's suggestion, they tried tying one end of the cable to a hammer and then throwing it again. But the hammer was too heavy. It plunged into the water and very nearly snagged the cable permanently on the bottom.

"*Not very bright, Nishikawa!*" Kelly Block called out from the other side of the water.

Data finally came up with the solution. There was a sharp bend in the creek farther up towards the hills. Data suggested that the team with the cable pay enough of it out to span the creek, strap the remaining coils to a board, and carry it up above the bend so that the flow of the water would carry it across the creek as it rounded the corner.

"Now *that*'s using your head!" Kelly Block called over.

"I'd like use this hammer on *his* head!" Nish hissed as he stood by Travis, watching the coils of cable head for the other bank.

Once the cable was across, they were able to mount it like a clothesline, running from one platform to the other. And finally, the Owls on Travis's side figured out how to fit little Simon Milliken into a safety harness and hang him from a sort of "roller skate" device they had fitted onto the cable. His teammates hoisted him up and launched him over the creek, little Simon sliding easily over the tumbling waters as Screech Owls on both sides cheered him on.

"Now *that*," a proud Kelly Block announced, "is teamwork."

It was, too. Travis felt great about what they had accomplished. They had been given a complicated problem and together they had solved it. Liz and Jesse had seen how to put the platforms together. Data had figured out how to get the cable across. Travis and Nish had worked on how to mount the cable onto the platforms. Jesse and Wilson had connected it all. Sarah had known how to work the safety harness. And Simon had flown over the river into the arms of the Owls on the other side – who had then used the same equipment to send Lars back.

"There was another way," Nish grumbled when all the team was once again gathered together.

"And what was that?" asked Kelly Block, suddenly interested.

Nish pointed up the slope, where a concrete bridge spanned the same swollen creek. "We could have driven."

Several of the Owls giggled, but Kelly Block just grimaced. Obviously, he and Nish weren't on the same wavelength when it came to humour – or, for that matter, hockey or anything else. If Block was looking for an example of "bad chemistry," Travis thought, he needed look no further than to Block himself and poor Nish.

Travis knew what was going on. He'd seen it too many times before. Nish was caught in a disaster of his own making. He was digging himself in deeper and deeper, desperately hoping his humour would spring him free when, in fact, it was only making matters worse.

Travis thought that perhaps Nish's luck had turned when Kelly Block announced that he was going to begin one-on-one sessions with the players. They were going to work on self-esteem and concentration and focus, and he was going to teach them some special "envisioning" techniques.

Those Owls who closely followed the NHL knew about "envisioning" and were excited by the prospect of learning how to do it themselves. Paul Kariya, who was idolized by many of the Owls – especially Nish, who still claimed Kariya was a distant "cousin" – was famous for his ability to concentrate fully on the game at hand. Even before a game began, he could "see" the way it would be played, and to the Screech Owls this ability was almost as impressive as his ability to skate so fast and shoot so quickly.

"We're going to do this step by step," Kelly Block announced. "We'll work on those things that distract you and keep you from being the player you can be, and then we're going to work on clearing your mind of everything but the game. We all start *envisioning* the same game; we all start *playing* the same game. And that's where proper team chemistry begins – *up here.*" Block tapped his forefinger against his right temple and spun slowly around on his heels so the point was made to every person in the room.

"I've drawn up a list of players in the order I'd like to meet with you," Block said. "You'll find it tacked up at the end of the hall."

The Owls rushed away to see, as if they were racing to slap a teammate who had just scored. Everyone wanted to know when they were going to start learning how to "envision." And everybody wanted to know who was going first.

The most surprised player of all, when they saw the list, was the one whose name was at the very top.

Wayne Nishikawa.

Travis was in his room, changing, when Nish burst in from his session with Kelly Block.

"*This guy is a certifiable class-A nut!*" Nish shouted, flopping backwards onto his unmade bed.

"Whadya mean?"

Nish sat up, his face red and flustered. "Okay," he said, "we go over my 'psychological profile,' right?"

"Right."

"He says I'm an insecure kid who has no sense of himself and doesn't even like himself. That's crap! I LOVE myself!"

Travis couldn't argue with Nish. But he couldn't really argue with Kelly Block, either. The truth, he figured, was somewhere in between.

"He wants me to refocus. He says I play the

wrong position for my personality. He says I'm a natural forward and that Muck has messed me up by having me always back on defence."

Travis shook his head in sympathy. "You've always played defence. Muck didn't put you there. He just kept you there."

"I know that. But this lunatic says that I have these *needs* that would make me a great forward. I *need* recognition. I *need* to be the star. I *need* to hear my name coming over the public-address system."

All true, Travis thought to himself. But he said nothing. And Nish didn't seem to see any truth in it. He continued, unaware that Travis was stifling a smile.

"So he says he's going to teach me how to 'envision' playing forward. He has me lie down on a couch while he plays this stupid sleepy music like my mother plays, and he tells me to close my eyes while he talks."

"Did you?"

"You have to — wait'll you get in there with him. It's creepy. He's a wacko!"

"Maybe."

"He sits there talking like he's me. You wouldn't believe it! He's sitting there saying, 'I want people to like me. I know my role on the team is to be the funny guy and make people laugh, but I don't really want to do that —'"

"But you do, too!"

"I know that. But he's being me, and he's not doing a very good job, okay. He's saying, 'I want to be Wayne Nishikawa, team leader. I want to be Wayne Nishikawa, good friend. I want to be Wayne Nishikawa, good person' – That's *him* speaking, not *me*. I just want to be Nish, and I'm not too crazy about being a good person!"

"What then?"

"What then? I don't know. I fell asleep."

Travis couldn't help himself. He started to laugh. "*You fell asleep?*"

"Yeah. So what?"

"How could you?"

"It was hot in there. And he had that awful music on. And he was getting pretty boring –"

"*You fell asleep!*" Travis repeated, delighted.

"Big deal. I'm awake now."

"Where was he when you woke up?"

"I don't know. Gone."

"He was *gone?*"

"Yeah. So?"

Travis couldn't believe it. Here was Kelly Block, trying to do what he was being paid to do, trying to do what he was supposed to be an expert in, and the kid he's working on falls fast asleep when he's talking to him.

"He must hate your guts," Travis said.

"Then we're even," Nish said. "Because I hate his."

6

TRAVIS AND LARS WERE COMING BACK FROM breakfast when they looked up the highway and saw a distant figure, furiously pedalling a mountain bike towards the camp.

"That's not who I think it is, is it?" said Travis.

"It is," said Lars. "Don't tell me Nish is finally trying to get in shape."

Nish was now in full view. His red face sweat-covered and blotched. He skidded in the gravel as he turned hard off the highway, straightened out and bolted through the gates to Camp Victory. He sagged on the handlebars as the bike rolled to a stop near the garage, his chest heaving as he gasped desperately for air.

"He's hyperventilating!" shouted Lars as the two Owls ran towards their friend.

"No he's not," corrected Travis. "Something's scared him!"

Travis knew his best friend well enough to know when Nish was badly frightened. Usually Nish was cocky and full of himself, but every once in a while he got scared into dropping the act and the little boy inside him came out.

45

"What's wrong?" Travis called as he and Lars raced up. He held the handlebars of the bike as Nish, unsteadily, dismounted and gulped air into his lungs. Travis noticed that Nish's T-shirt and track pants were soaked through with sweat.

"You okay?" asked Lars.

Nish gasped and choked and spat and moaned. He fell to his knees and placed both hands on the ground in front of him, hanging his head as he fought for air and calm.

"*Nish!*" Travis finally demanded. "*Tell us what's wrong!*"

Nish looked up, his face swollen and soaked. Tears? Sweat? Travis couldn't tell.

"You, you . . . won't . . . b–b–believe m–me!" Nish gasped.

"Believe what?" Lars asked. He was gently patting Nish's back, trying to offer him some comfort.

Nish stared hard at them, his eyes pleading for them to take him seriously. Travis had never seen such desperation in his friend's eyes. The look alone scared him – and he didn't even know what it was that had frightened Nish!

"I s–saw . . . some . . . thing," Nish gulped. He seemed about to break into tears.

"What?" Travis asked. "What did you see?" There couldn't be grizzlies around here, could there? And there weren't any buffalo around any

46

more, were there? Except in special parks. Nish couldn't have started a stampede, could he?

But Nish wasn't saying. He seemed to have caught his breath now, but he was strangely silent. This wasn't Nish, Travis thought to himself. Nish was the one who always had to tell everything, first and loudest if possible.

Nish spoke in a very quiet voice. "You won't . . . believe me."

"Try us," suggested Lars. He had a look of utter sincerity on his face. Travis was glad it was Lars who was there with him. Nish could trust Lars the same as he could trust his closest friend, Travis.

"What?" Travis asked.

They helped Nish over to the steps of the nearest cabin. He sat quietly until he had his breath back, then tried to remain calm as he told them what had happened.

The night before, Nish hadn't been able to fall asleep. He had tossed and turned all through the night. He had tried every trick he knew – counting sheep, counting goals, dreaming up gross tricks to play on his teammates – but nothing worked. All he could think about was the look in Kelly Block's eyes as the so-called sports expert told him that he, Wayne Nishikawa, all-star defence at the Quebec City International Peewee Tournament, all-star defence at the Lake

Placid International Peewee Hockey Championship, was now supposed to be a forward!

He got up and went to the open window. Everything here was upside down. Defence to forward. Winter to summer.

Nish stared out towards the hills. There was a faint ribbon of red on the high ledge; dawn creeping into the valley. There was no point in sleeping now. No point in even trying.

He had thought of waking Travis up, but Travis was so deep in sleep, Nish was torn between waking him up and doing something funny to him. He thought a dirty trick might perk him up, and headed back to his duffel bag for his special can of shaving cream that had come on every trip Nish had made with the Screech Owls.

He tiptoed back to Travis's bedside and very carefully squeezed out a long unicorn horn of cream on Travis's forehead, teasing and twisting the pile so high that it held just a moment before drooping down over Travis's nose and mouth. Travis, still fast asleep, swatted at the irritation and rolled over, spreading shaving cream all over his pillow.

But Nish couldn't even force a smile. He just wasn't his old self.

He put the shaving cream carefully away – stopping first to fill one of Lars's boots – and sat on the edge of his rumpled bed, trying to decide what to do.

He started to dress, pulling on his Screech Owls sweatpants, a T-shirt, and his Owls windbreaker. If the warm gust from the window was any hint of the day to come, he wouldn't need anything else.

He had no idea what he would do. He didn't want to hang around the camp – Camp Defeat, he was starting to call it – in case Mental Block was also up early and the two of them bumped into each other. Nish wouldn't mind bumping into Block – but only if he, Nish, was driving a train.

He had it in his mind that he had to get away. And the only way to do that was to take one of the mountain bikes and head off for a while into the Badlands. He liked the name – it seemed like a place where he would belong.

Nish slipped out quietly, easing the door shut so that no one would awake. He stepped carefully, avoiding the creaky board on the steps and jumping down from the cabin onto the soft sand that had appeared as the snow ran off towards the river.

There was no lock on the garage that held the mountain bikes. Nish wondered, briefly, how many places there were left in the world like Drumheller and at home in Tamarack, where you didn't need to lock up everything you owned if you ever expected to see it again. He liked this town. He just didn't like Kelly Block and Camp Defeat.

Nish eased out the best bike within reach – a Gary Fisher, with front and rear suspension and a built-in computer that would tell him not only how far he had gone but how long he'd gone. He was sort of running away, but his stomach was already rumbling with demands for breakfast. He'd just go for a little while, and be back in time to put the bike away and meet the rest of the guys back at the cabin before breakfast.

No, on second thought he'd better just meet them *at* breakfast – Travis and Lars would want to get him back for the shaving cream!

It was beautiful out on the highway. The sky to the east was blue and gold and pink, and the thin light of dawn gave the few houses along the way a blue-black tint, as if they were silhouettes rather than houses. Already there were some people up, and the lights in upstairs rooms gave strange cat's eyes to some of the buildings.

He rode hard until he got to Rosedale and the suspension footbridge. He knew there were good paths on the other side. He tried riding his bike across the bridge, but the swinging motion made his balance uncertain, so he got off and walked, staring down through the steel-grate floor of the bridge at the churning grey-brown water. Any higher, he thought, and he wouldn't have the stomach to make this crossing.

There were no houses on the other side. There had once been an old coal mine, but it was long since abandoned, and though there were signs saying "PRIVATE PROPERTY" bike trails headed off everywhere, disappearing behind the shoulders of the sandhills. There were supposed to be more hoodoos back here – perhaps he'd find some.

Back on his bike, Nish headed into the Badlands. He was breathing hard, pumping determinedly as the bike darted along the trails, the shocks cushioning every small bump and washout. He was alone in the middle of what seemed like nowhere, and he felt completely at ease. It surprised him and pleased him that he felt this way.

He looked around at the barren hills and the strange rock formations. It was no longer the age of TV and video games and McDonald's. It felt as if he had gone back a hundred million years in time. And he was the only human on the face of Earth!

Nish giggled to himself. He was no twelve-year-old kid on the run from Camp Defeat, he was the ferocious Deinonychus they had talked about at the museum. He had the greatest eye-sight of all the dinosaurs. He was quickest on his feet, fastest with his hands. No, not hands – long claws, sharp as scalpels. He chomped his teeth together, imagining they were twice the size of a shark's, and ten times as sharp.

The path Nish had taken through the hills rose and fell. He had to keep changing gears and, at times, his rear wheel spun with the extra energy he seemed to have found, small pebbles flying out behind him. He looked back, admiring his own dust. A dust cloud in March, in Canada. Incredible.

Nish was beginning to feel much better. *Why feel sorry for myself*, he wondered, *when the real fool here is Mental Block?* Why worry about anything when he could ride a bike so nice in country like this? The air was warm in his face and fresh with the start of the day. If this was indeed what the world was like at the dawn of history, then he wouldn't mind being there at all.

Nish stood on his pedals to accelerate up a steep incline. The front wheel of the bike rose and twisted in the air. The rear wheel spun hard, jumping the bike hard.

What was that sound?

Nish let the bike settle and put one foot on the ground, turning back to see what had made that strange throaty sound behind him.

Was it the rear wheel catching? Was it a bird? An animal?

Nish shivered. But it wasn't cold. It was warm, probably heading for hot. He was sweating – but now the sweat felt like little chips of ice running down his back and under his arms.

One hundred million years collapsed in a second. Nish was no longer all alone in the pre-historic world of the dinosaurs; he was all alone in the modern world of the Badlands.

And he was scared.

The noise came again. It sounded like it came from a cave. It sounded like it came from some great pit that had no bottom.

The mine? Weren't there still old mine shafts around here?

But what was making the sound? There were all sorts of animals in the West that Nish didn't know anything about. He'd never seen a coyote. He'd never even seen a prairie dog until Andy pointed them out as the bus made its way along the highway from Calgary.

But wouldn't a coyote howl? This was no howl – it was a growl!

Nish got off his bike and stood by it, thinking that in case of an attack he might keep the bike between him and whatever animal it was out there with him.

Nish began to whimper. He began to wish he hadn't made fun of the Little Church. He might need divine help here, and what if there was a Big God and a Big Jesus standing up in the clouds somewhere, remembering that Nish had insulted their church and joked about them being little, and had decided that, as far as they were concerned, Nish was on his own.

"H–help me!" he whined.

Nish realized he had spoken out loud and instantly regretted it. What if someone had heard? What if the sound had come from one of the Owls, getting him back for the shaving cream.

Maybe they'd heard him and were standing behind that closest hill, laughing at him right now.

What if it was Kelly Block? What if he'd followed Nish out and now knew what a great big chicken Nish could be when it came down to the crunch?

If someone was indeed watching, Nish couldn't betray his own terror. He had to act brave. His reputation might depend on it. He told himself to remember what Mr. Imoo had taught him in Nagano: to be a Samurai Warrior, to fear nothing. He owed it to his old friend to at least try.

He decided to walk towards the sound.

It had come from behind him, down and to the left, probably from behind that twisted hoodoo that looked like a giant pink-and-brown toadstool.

Nish turned his bike and straddled it, coasting down with his toes clicking the earth and the brakes on, ready to bolt at the slightest sign of a coyote.

"W—who's there?" he called, weakly.

Again, a throaty roar! Louder this time.

Nish had never heard such a sound. It sounded like it came from a sewer – or a crypt. Nish had never heard a sound from a crypt. He had never even seen a crypt! But he had seen enough horror movies to know that a sound from a crypt is blood-curdling and filled with all kinds of horrors, from rotting skulls with squashed eyes to hideous snakes and bats and spiders and slugs and maggots and . . .

Nish shook his head sharply. *Idiot*, he said to himself, *you're letting your imagination run away on you! Get a grip! It's one of the team. Or it's nothing. It's probably nothing.*

Nish rolled farther down the hill, coming to a stop in front of the hoodoo. He waited, listening. Nothing. Dead quiet.

A shadow moved!

Nish felt his heart in his throat. He felt it choking him. He could hardly keep a grip on the handlebars his arms were shaking so badly.

"W—who's th—there?" he asked in a small, shaking voice.

Nothing.

The shadow moved again! Large. Huge. And right behind the hoodoo!

Nish lifted his feet onto the pedals. He flicked the gears down to first, in case he had to jump fast. He pedalled ahead, silently, carefully, easing closer to the other side of the hoodoo.

"T—Travis!" he called. But there was no answer. "M—Mr. B—Block?" He was near tears, biting his lip hard.

THE GROWL ALMOST KNOCKED HIM OVER!

Nish leaped high on his seat and hammered down hard on the pedal, his foot slipping off and the rear wheel digging in sharp and failing to catch on the loose gravel. He lost it, and the bike went down, Nish spilling off the seat, over the handlebars, rolling on the sharp stones.

He lay on his back, wild with panic. He turned his head back towards the growl.

The shadow moved again!

And suddenly, from behind the hoodoo, a huge head emerged.

A head as big as the body that followed!

Huge teeth flashing, darting tongue!

Massive scales, rising like little horns along the nose and around the eye!

Green and brown and red and speckled!

Small shrunken hands, with claws like knives!

And a long tail, whipping slowly, menacingly!

The head turned – a small, green, beady eye sizing up its victim!

"I'M SO SORRY, GOD!" Nish screamed.

"Help me!

"Help me!

"HELLLLLLLLLPPPPPP MEEEEEEEEEEEEEEEEEE!"

Nish sighed deeply and looked up at Travis and Lars.

Travis couldn't help himself. A smile quick as a blink flickered on his mouth – and Nish caught it.

"*I knew you wouldn't believe me!*" he wailed. "*No one will believe me!*"

"We didn't say we didn't believe you," argued Travis. "It's just that . . ."

Nish stared back hard, defiant. "Just what?

Just that dinosaurs don't exist anymore, is that it?"

"Well . . ."

"Maybe you just saw something like a dinosaur," suggested Lars. "A big shadow, or something."

"I told you. I *did* see a shadow. But then I saw it, face to face."

"What kind?" Travis asked.

"One of those things that looks like the Tyrannosaurus rex — the one from around here."

"Albertosaurus," Lars said.

It wasn't possible. Travis racked his brains trying to think what Nish *might* have seen, might have thought he saw. There were all kinds of phony dinosaurs around Drumheller, on street corners and in parks. The realistic, life-size replicas — including one Albertosaurus in attack mode — outside the main building of the Royal Tyrrell Museum. But Nish was nowhere near there!

"You're sure you went right, not left towards town?"

"I guess I know where I was," Nish said defiantly.

Travis and Lars looked at each other quickly. They had indeed seen him pedalling hard from the east, where the hoodoos were located.

"Nish . . . ," Lars began.

"*What?*" Nish almost shouted. He was angry, impatient. Perhaps he felt he should never have told them.

"This isn't another one of your famous tricks, is it?"

Nish wrenched the bike away from them and threw it to the ground. "Oh, go to hell if you won't believe me," he shouted, his voice choking. "I'm telling you the truth."

Nish walked away, head down, then turned on them, face again swollen and red.

"I SAW A DINOSAUR! A REAL, LIVE DINOSAUR!"

And then he turned and bolted.

7

"I THINK IT WAS THE WIND."

Travis couldn't follow Lars's argument. Lars was saying that maybe the chinook had somehow addled Nish's brain. He said there was a similar wind in Europe, the *föhn*, and it was famous for the effect it had on people's minds. Some people, he claimed, even killed themselves when the warm *föhn* began blowing north across the Mediterranean from North Africa in what should have been the dead of winter. Perhaps Nish had just been struck with a similar kind of sudden terror while out on the trail, Lars suggested, and had imagined an Albertosaurus because he'd seen the Royal Tyrrell model just the day before.

"Maybe," Travis said. But he wasn't convinced.

There seemed no rational answer. Nish could act the fool, but he wasn't a fool. Nish loved tricks, but he wouldn't trick about something like this. He knew Nish well enough to know that Nish had been terrified, frightened as badly here in Drumheller as he had been that time in James

Bay when they'd been lost in the woods at night and Nish had dreamed he was being attacked by the Trickster and had wet his sleeping bag.

Whatever had really happened, Lars and Travis decided to keep Nish's story to themselves. Nish had been so frustrated he'd gone to his room after breakfast complaining of a headache so severe he couldn't make the exercise class that was about to start. When Kelly Block heard the news, it seemed as if he was somehow satisfied. Maybe he thought Nish was reacting to hearing the sad truth about his personality.

Nish had said nothing more. And neither Travis nor Lars would say anything until they had a better idea of what had happened to their friend on his dawn bicycle ride. Besides, even if they had told the rest of the Screech Owls that Nish had seen a living, breathing dinosaur, it would have paled against the topic that was currently holding the Owls spellbound.

The new team roster.

Kelly Block had posted it while Ty was leading the team through a light workout in the main yard of Camp Victory. It was Sarah who saw it first when they came into the camp kitchen for a short break and some Gatorade.

She wasted no words in her response: "Is this a joke?"

But it was not a joke. Based on his "psychological profiles" and interviews with the players,

Kelly Block had designed a roster that he claimed would result in "improved team chemistry."

Sarah Cuthbertson was now playing left defence.

Wayne Nishikawa had become a centre.

Travis Lindsay was on right wing, not left.

Dmitri Yakushev, the quickest skater on the team, was now a penalty killer.

Fahd Noorizadeh, who scored about once every twenty games, was on the power play.

And so it went. Those who were defence were now mostly forwards. Scorers were now checkers. Checkers were now scorers. The only positions that hadn't changed were Jeremy and Jenny in goal, but the way Kelly Block was going about redesigning the Screech Owls, maybe Mr. Dillinger would be in net for the next game.

Travis felt as if his world was spinning out of control. The other players were turning to him, as their captain, in the hope that he might have some answers.

He felt he needed to talk to Muck – but Muck wasn't here. He couldn't even talk to his parents. They weren't here, either. The only Screech Owls parent, apart from Mr. Dillinger, who'd made the trip to Alberta was Mr. Higgins – and Kelly Block was his idea! As for Ty and Mr. Dillinger, both of them seemed overwhelmed by Block's bully tactics and his energetic way of taking charge of everything that happened at Camp Victory.

"I don't mind," said Fahd.

"You're on the power play," said Derek. "Why should you?"

"I'm going to refuse to dress," said Lars, who was now a forward.

"We have to," said Travis. "We're guests here. We can't ruin the tournament just because of Mental Block."

"*No way!* Absolutely no way! I won't. I won't."

"You have to."

Travis was alone with his friend, but getting nowhere. Nish was still in his bed, his pillow pulled down over his face, the covers up to his neck, as if he was expecting snakes to come pouring in under the door. Travis wondered how Nish could stand it. It was boiling hot in the cabin, the chinook still burning down from the hills.

"Look," Travis finally said, "you've got to think about the team, not Mental Block. We're the Screech Owls and we have to show up. We always show up."

"We're not the Screech Owls. He's turned us into a bunch of turkeys."

"It won't work. He'll start out with his new line-up and it won't work, and before you know it you'll be back on defence and Sarah will be back on forward and we'll be the Owls again. You just wait and see."

"You're wrong," Nish said, lowering the pillow just enough to look out with one eye. "You're wrong and I'll prove you're wrong."

"How?"

"I'll go, okay? And I'll play. And you watch. He's too stubborn to change his mind."

Game two was against the Winnipeg Werewolves, a good-but-not-great peewee team from Manitoba that would normally have been hard pressed to stay within three goals of the Screech Owls, let alone beat them.

But this was no longer the Screech Owls. This was confusion.

Kelly Block was now firmly in place as the lead coach of the Owls. Ty was plainly very upset, but, really, Ty was still just a kid himself. He was only a few years older than most of the Owls, and they looked up to him as a fine hockey player and an even better person, but he had no hope of standing up to the force of Kelly Block's personality. Neither did Mr. Dillinger, who was keeping very much to the background, sharpening skates and taping sticks and, for once, not smiling as he went about his job.

Mr. Higgins was no help, either. Poor Andy felt like he had to apologize for his father. "I'm sorry," he said to Travis at one point. "But my dad thinks Kelly Block walks on water."

"I know," said Travis. "Don't worry. We'll soon be back home and all this will have gone away."

But when he thought of Nish, Travis wasn't so sure. Some of the damage done there was going to take more than a flight back to Tamarack to cure. But he couldn't explain that to Andy. No one but Lars and Travis knew about Nish's strange mental state, which Travis thought was probably all due to Kelly Block. And no one but Lars and Travis would be able to help Nish get over it.

The Owls dressed for the game in disturbing silence. It seemed as if they weren't even breathing. Mr. Dillinger was keeping to himself, and Ty was nowhere to be seen.

Kelly Block looked as if he'd been waiting for this moment. He had on a suit, just like a coach in the big leagues, and a tie with so many cartoon characters on it, it looked more like a bad comic book than something anyone would ever wear. He had even been to town to get his hair cut.

"All right, now!" Block had shouted as he stood in the centre of the room. "This is a brand-new start for a brand-new team. We begin today to become the team we were always meant to be."

Travis heard Nish's sigh from the far corner. But no one raised a head.

"We're going to 'envision' this game right now," said Block. "When I stop speaking I want each and every one of you to see the game that's coming up. I want you to breathe the Werewolves. I want victory to be rushing through your blood. I want the Screech Owls to be the only thought that's in your head – the Screech Owls, victorious. Understand?"

He stopped speaking. In the sudden silence Travis was aware of his own breathing. The silence descended in layers, building on them until he wanted to scream.

He wondered if anyone was actually "envisioning" the upcoming game against the Werewolves. *He* couldn't. He didn't think Nish could. He figured his brain and Nish's brain were locked onto the same image – and it had nothing to do with any hockey game.

It was of a monstrous creature that hadn't been seen for a hundred million years.

The game against Winnipeg could not have gone worse. Nish lost every faceoff he took. Sarah got caught out of position on two goals. Fahd had a breakaway on the power play and missed the net. Lars had trouble reading the play. Travis, forgetting that he was now a right-winger, kept crisscrossing at centre ice and bumping into the left-winger, leaving the right side open for every rush the Werewolves cared to start.

If it hadn't been for Jenny and Jeremy, who split the game in net, the score would have been even worse than it was. But in the end the Winnipeg Werewolves had five goals, the Screech Owls only three.

It was the worst team they had ever lost to.

8

THE ONE–ON–ONE SESSIONS WITH KELLY BLOCK were over. A few of the Owls, like Fahd, had actually enjoyed them. Fahd said Block had made him feel better about himself and his role on the Screech Owls. Others had hated their time with the sports psychologist – but no one as much as Nish.

Kelly Block was trying to work on the team's "chemistry," Travis reminded himself. Well, he supposed there was good chemistry and bad chemistry. He remembered Mr. Hepburn, the science teacher back home, demonstrating how some things mix and others do not. Mr. Hepburn had sprinkled salt into a beaker of water, and the class had watched as the granules dissolved and were soon, with some stirring, gone altogether – the salty taste the only evidence that anything had been added. Then Mr. Hepburn had taken a small, seemingly harmless piece of material called magnesium and, using forceps to carry it and wearing protective glasses over his eyes, had dropped the tiniest piece into the water – and the explosion had shattered the beaker!

Kelly Block and Nish, Travis supposed, were a bit like water and magnesium.

The morning after the disastrous game against the Werewolves, Kelly Block had summoned six players to his office: Travis, Sarah, Lars, Jesse, Andy, and Jenny. A goaltender and five players – a full unit.

He brought them into a room off his office, a room with bean-bag chairs and soft couches and thick rugs. He suggested they stretch out and relax.

Travis lay on one of the rugs, looking up at the slowly turning ceiling fan and trying to see into the main office. Kelly Block certainly had all the best equipment for running Camp Victory. There were computers and video monitors and bookcases stretching around most of the room. There were model airplanes and model birds hanging from the ceiling, and a miniature basketball net against the door and two small basketballs carefully set on Kelly Block's big black desk. Everything – paper, books, tapes – was in perfect order.

"You may wonder why you six are here," Block began.

No one said a word.

"That's why we do our psychological testing," he continued. "The questions may not make any sense to you – I know, I giggled too, the first time I saw some of them – but in the end you cannot fool the system. If you answer the way you think

68

I want you to, you end up tricking yourself on the next question, and so on . . ."

Travis's mind had already begun to wander. He wondered if the others were listening. But he could see nothing but the big fan above his head slowly turning.

"I ran your sheets through the computer, did some number crunching, talked to each member of the team, and identified the six of you as team 'generators.' That's not quite the same thing as team 'leaders,' so don't get the wrong idea. You are all leaders, too, but more important, you generate the energy this team draws from. You inspire with your play. You motivate with your emotion. You command respect with your personality . . ."

Travis smiled smugly to himself. This wasn't so bad. He liked being a "generator."

"We have, gathered here, a goaltender, two defence and three forwards. The Russians, as you know, play the game in five-man — sorry, five-*person* — units, not defence pairings and forward lines. Better chemistry. I've identified Jenny as our goaltender of choice and you five as our premier unit."

"*Our?*" Travis wondered. *Since when did Kelly Block belong to the Screech Owls hockey team? And did he talk this way to all teams? What if Muck were here? What would he think? And where was Dmitri? How could Kelly Block dare call something a "Russian unit" and not include the only Russian on the team? And what of Jeremy? If Jenny was the "goaltender of choice," what was Jeremy? The goaltender of second choice?*

It was getting warm in the room. Kelly Block's voice began to take on a purring quality. The fan turned slowly, slowly . . .

Travis tried to stay with Kelly Block this time. He was talking about "generators" and "envisioning" and "imaging" and "focus," and Travis's own focus was beginning to slip again. He wondered how the others were hanging in, but he couldn't see anyone. And he didn't think he should turn his head or sit up to look. There could be no doubt that Kelly Block was sitting there, staring at the six of them, watching them . . .

"Let's head for the hoodoos!"

Sarah's suggestion had been enthusiastically endorsed by the rest of the "Unit," as the six Screech Owls were now referring to themselves. They had spent nearly two hours with Kelly Block and, Travis was pleased to note, Block had never realized that at least one of the Unit had dozed off in the middle of his presentation. Jesse claimed he, too, had fallen asleep. Jenny said she had just got bored and lost her train of thought.

They weren't much impressed with Kelly Block's inspirational address to the generators, but they did like his suggestion that they head out on the mountain bikes – just the six of them – for some critical "bonding" before the next game.

"If he wants us to bond," Andy said, "why doesn't he just glue us to each other?"

But Travis and Sarah knew what Kelly Block meant. Perhaps he had gone overboard, but there was something to be said for being a true team and having to depend on each other, whether falling backwards from a chair or breaking out of one's own end. A bike ride in the barren hills across the river seemed a perfectly good idea.

Travis and Lars exchanged a quick glance.

The hoodoos.

Where Nish had imagined he saw the Albertosaurus.

"Maybe we'll see a Tyrannosaurus rex," Lars whispered.

Travis giggled and kicked his pedal hard, doing a slight wheelie out onto the highway.

The air was warm on Travis's face. He felt happy with his friends – the Unit. He had almost forgotten about poor Nish's run-in with his own panicking imagination.

Poor Nish. Maybe they'd be able to see whatever it was that he had taken for an Albertosaurus.

Maybe they'd be able to show him that it had been nothing but his mind playing tricks on him.

Was it warm enough, Travis wondered, for Nish to have seen a mirage?

9

THE CHINOOK WAS HOLDING. THE WIND WAS running through the valley like hot air through a heating duct, the river swollen and the ground so quickly dry that small lassos of dust flew up from their tires as they rode off the highway towards the suspension bridge that would take them into the rolling hills and the magnificent, eerie hoodoos.

Travis felt great. The wind was in his face. He had an excellent mountain bike under him. He was taking the runs easily, gearing down for the rises effortlessly. He had a natural eye for reading terrain and moved quicker, more sure, than any of the others. He had forgotten all about Nish and his wild story. He had forgotten all about Kelly Block and his chemistry. He had forgotten about the loss to the Werewolves.

It was so good to be out here with his friends. Sarah was right alongside him, as graceful and sure-footed on a mountain bike as she was on a hockey rink. Lars was letting his back wheel drift around corners, causing Jesse to scream that he was going to lose it, but Lars never did. Andy was strong going up the hills, cautious going down. Jenny was exactly the same on the trails as she was in net: steady.

Deeper and deeper into the Badlands they went. Strange rock formations rose all about them, casting long, bizarrely shaped shadows on each other and along the curling, twisting trails. There was a sense of other-worldliness here. It felt like a different planet, a different time.

Now Travis's thoughts did return to Nish. He could see how someone with a vivid imagination – and Nish had one of the wildest – might think he had seen anything here from giant toadstools to alien statues.

Some of the sandstone structures even had faces – if you looked at a certain angle.

What was that sound?

Sarah had moved ahead of Travis on the flat, and dust rose sharply as she braked. Travis braked hard and turned, his rear wheel digging in and sliding to a fast stop. The others braked hard, dust rolling all around them, blocking any clear view.

"Did you hear that?" Sarah asked.

"I heard something," Travis said.

"I heard it, too," said Andy. "What was it?"

"Sounded like a sick lion," suggested Lars.

"There's no lions in Alberta," said Jenny. Travis could detect a little shiver in her voice.

Again, the same sound – closer!

Sarah turned sharply, ready to pump. "*What the – ?*"

"*My God!*" Andy called out. "L–L–L–OOK!"

Travis turned to follow Andy's line of vision. His eyes moved along the grey-brown trail past a small hoodoo and came to a break between two steeply sloping hills.

What he saw first was the movement – a tail lashing back and forth in the space between the slopes as something moved from shadow to light.

Something with small beady red eyes.

Something with huge horn-like scales about the eye and down the neck.

Something red and rust and dirt yellow and dull green.

Something huge.

And something impossible!

An Albertosaurus!

"It's a trick!" Travis said, but he didn't even sound convincing to himself.

"*It's coming at us!*" Jenny squealed.

It could not be a model; it moved. It could not be a balloon; the ground rumbled as it stepped. It could not be a trick of their eyes; it roared, and their ears filled with a sound unlike anything any of them had heard before.

It was a sound that seemed to come from the centre of the earth itself.

The monster stepped again towards them and the ground around them trembled!

As a perfect unit, the six Screech Owls turned on their bikes, leapt high above their seats, and pushed down so hard on their pedals that six back wheels spun uselessly in the dirt. A dustcloud rose so high and thick around them that, when Travis looked back, he could barely make out the shadow of the dinosaur.

But it was still there, tail lashing, eyes flashing, tongue flicking. The monster hurled a mighty roar at them, and lowered its head as if preparing to charge.

"GO!" Andy called.

"RUN FOR IT!" Sarah shouted.

"HELLLLLP!" Jesse screamed.

"HELLLLLLP UUUUSSSSSSSS!"

10

"I *TOLD* YOU SO."

Travis didn't need to hear this from Nish, but he supposed Nish had to hear himself say it. Nish *had* told them so — and Travis and Lars had dismissed the story as a trick of Nish's overactive imagination.

But now Travis knew that what Nish had seen was real.

There was no keeping secrets this time. The six Owls who had headed out into the Badlands to bond together as a unit had become witnesses to the most extraordinary story to hit the town of Drumheller since 1884, when a young geologist names J.B. Tyrrell climbed one of these strange hills and came face to face with the seventy-million-year-old skull of an Albertosaurus.

It seemed impossible, but now, more than a century later, six kids from a peewee hockey team had found another Albertosaurus — and this one was alive!

Make that seven kids. Nish had already begun to claim his rightful place at centre stage.

"I found it first," he told anyone who would listen.

Unfortunately for the Screech Owls, a great many people wanted to listen. The six Screech Owls who thought they had seen a living dinosaur had come flying back to Camp Victory in such a panic and with so many shouts for help that there was no keeping this a secret. Jenny and Lars had both thrown up they'd been so frightened, and Andy couldn't talk when his father began yelling at him to tell him what had happened. Finally, Sarah and Travis managed to force the story out, in the midst of gasps and sobs from their teammates.

Someone must have made a call, for within half an hour a reporter from the local newspaper, the *Drumheller Mail*, was at the camp gate. An hour later the *Calgary Herald* was there demanding interviews with the kids who claimed they'd seen a living dinosaur. And not much later people from the wire services and television stations had flooded the town.

And then came the Royal Canadian Mounted Police.

Mr. Higgins and Kelly Block met the police car at the front gate and let them in. On Block's insistence, the television cameras had not been allowed through, but they were set up anyway all along the edge of the highway, filming anything that moved and calling questions over the fence to any Screech Owl who happened to walk between cabins.

"DID YOU SEE THE DINOSAUR?"

"CAN YOU TALK TO US?"

"WHERE ARE THE KIDS WHO SAY THEY SAW THE MONSTER?"

On Mr. Higgins's advice, the Owls didn't try to answer the reporters' questions. The police were there, he said, and the police would take charge of matters.

After an hour or so, it struck Travis as odd that the most natural thing to do had not been done – or even suggested.

"Why aren't they going into the hills to look for it?" he said to Sarah.

"They don't believe us," she said.

"They think we made it up," said Lars.

"I know what I saw," said Nish, growing prouder by the moment. "I know what I saw, and I know what it was."

Nish wanted to go out to the fence and talk to the camera crews, but the other Owls wouldn't let him. They milled around the kitchen area, waiting to see what the Mounties and other adults would decide to do. For the first time since he had met him, Travis began to feel sorry for Kelly Block. All this attention couldn't be doing his camp much good.

There were now many more people here than

just the police. Some looked like scientists. They had gathered with Kelly Block in a meeting room to discuss the situation. Sarah went over and sat close to the door, trying to hear what was being said inside.

She soon reported back, unimpressed.

"They think it has something to do with the chinook," she said. "There's a guy with them who I think might be a psychiatrist. He's talking about 'mass hysteria' and things like that. He says we suffered some kind of 'gang delusion.'"

"What language are you talking?" demanded Nish.

Fahd, who knew something about everything, explained. "He thinks you all dreamed the same thing at the same time."

"That's impossible!" said Andy.

"No," said Fahd. "It can happen. Lots of experts think that's what UFOs are. Somebody thinks they see a flying saucer, and suddenly everybody in town thinks they see them."

"We don't *think* we saw anything," said Nish a bit testily. "We did see a dinosaur. And *I* saw it first!"

11

BY MORNING, THE STORY WAS OUT OF CONTROL. The claim of the six kids – "*Seven*," Nish kept correcting – who said they had seen a living, breathing dinosaur had travelled around the world. American stations were sending in television crews. CNN was on the scene, broadcasting live. The Screech Owls were headline news, but it was hardly the kind of publicity they might once have dreamed of as they headed into a hockey tournament:

"CANADIAN CHILDREN TELL MONSTER FIB!"

"TINY HOCKEY PLAYERS ATTEMPT PREHISTORIC HOAX"

"CHINOOK BLAMED FOR YOUNGSTERS' WILD CLAIM"

"FAIRIES AND FLYING SAUCERS – NOW LIVING, BREATHING DINOSAURS!"

"TERROR IN THE BADLANDS!"

Their parents had all phoned. Some of them were beside themselves with worry. Sarah's mother had been in tears. Travis's father had told him to remain calm, to say only what he knew to be a fact, and not to be afraid of the truth. Nish asked his mom to clip out all the newspaper stories.

The angle that most of the media had taken concerned children making up stories to draw attention to themselves. One story cited dozens of examples of stories where youngsters had fabricated huge lies and fooled their families and everyone else, at least for a while, and sometimes for years. Many of the news reports compared the "Drumheller Dinosaur Sighting" to an event that took place in England back in 1920. Two little girls who lived in a village in Yorkshire claimed to have played with real fairies since they were tiny, and had been able to take two photographs of the tiny flying creatures with a camera. The story had been such a sensation, and so many people had believed the two girls and their photographic evidence, that even the famous writer Arthur Conan Doyle, creator of the Sherlock Holmes mysteries, was called upon to give his opinion. The great man gave his backing to the little girls' amazing story. The hoax was not revealed for decades, when one of the little girls, now a very old woman, decided she could not go to her grave carrying such a fib.

There were no photographs of the Alberta dinosaur, all the stories gleefully pointed out.

"No one believes us," Sarah said despondently.

The police briefly interviewed the seven Screech Owls, and one of the Mounties, who seemed very cross with them, warned that they could be charged with public mischief if they didn't own up to the truth.

"This is a very serious charge, young ladies and gentlemen," he said. "It would be a most serious blemish on your record and your families' good names."

"But it's the *truth*!" said an exasperated Lars. "We saw a real, live dinosaur."

"*I* saw it first," added Nish.

If the reporters and the Mounties didn't believe the Screech Owls, there were soon lots of others who did. Within a day Drumheller was flooded with the curious. Before long there wasn't a vacant hotel room to be found between Drumheller and Calgary. They arrived first from all over Canada and the United States, and in the days after from England and France and Germany and Japan . . .

Several of the supermarket tabloid papers then hit the stands with stories – including photographs! – that seemed to back the seven kids' version of what had happened. One of these papers even had a front-page headline that claimed, "CANADIAN AUTHORITIES DESPERATE TO SUPPRESS KIDS' DISCOVERY OF THE MILLENNIUM!"

Using their Walkmans, the Owls were able to hear some of the debate on the local radio talk shows. Most of the discussion involved dinosaur jokes at the expense of the Screech Owls, but several callers seemed to think that this extraordinary chinook had somehow, in some unknown way, released a slumbering, frozen giant from prehistory. Fahd was quick to point out that this explanation didn't make sense – but then, what part of the story did make sense? All they knew for sure was that it had somehow captured the imagination of a good part of the world.

Traffic out to the Badlands became so frantic that the RCMP put up roadblocks and declared the barren hills beyond the suspension bridge off-limits – which only served to convince many that there really was something out there.

It seemed insanity had come to Dinosaur Valley. European television crews rented helicopters and were even flying about at night with huge searchlights bouncing over the hills. Hikers were walking in from the opposite direction, ignoring the roadblocks.

And hour by hour, the Mounties were getting angrier with the seven hockey players who refused to back down on their story. There was even a rumour that the seven youngsters were about to be formally charged with public mischief.

Mr. Higgins, looking very worried, gathered the seven Owls in the camp meeting room. He had Kelly Block with him and another man, Mr. Banning, who was a Calgary lawyer.

"The police are getting very concerned that this has gone too far," the lawyer said. "I happen to know they are right now preparing charges against you."

"They should be out looking for the Albertosaurus," said Sarah, "not worrying about us."

"Well, miss," said the lawyer. Travis glanced at Sarah and saw her grimace; Sarah hated to be called "miss." The lawyer didn't even notice. "Well, miss, they are indeed worried about you," he continued. "I have been asked by them if perhaps you would all, or even a couple of you, be willing to undergo lie-detector tests."

The Owls looked at each other.

"That proves they don't believe us!" said Nish.

Sarah shook her head. "But it also gives us a chance to prove we're telling the truth."

"Let's do it," said Lars.

"I don't know, son," cautioned Mr. Higgins. He seemed distinctly uncomfortable with the idea.

"Come on, Dad," said Andy. "Or don't you believe us, either?"

Mr. Higgins stumbled and mumbled. It was clear that he did not.

"I'll do it," said Travis.

"So will I," said Nish.

All around the circle, the Owls nodded their agreement.

12

PERHAPS, TRAVIS THOUGHT, THIS WAS WHY television broadcasters called big games "The Moment of Truth." He knew that he and the other Screech Owls had won the battle of the lie-detector test – the green line never jumped for any of them, at least when it mattered – and now they would have to win the battle of game three of the Drumheller Invitational.

The tournament wasn't about to stop just because the town had filled up with news reporters and the curious. There was still a schedule to be played out and a trophy to be won. The Screech Owls, however, seemed hardly in the running any more. Lose this game, and they would be headed home, with nothing to show for their trip but a bunch of newspaper clippings about an imaginary dinosaur.

The opposition was, appropriately, called the Predators. The Prince Albert Predators from northern Saskatchewan. They were, by all accounts, a good team, strong up centre and solid in goal. In any other circumstance, the Screech

Owls versus the Predators would have been a great match.

But these were hardly normal circumstances. The little Drumheller arena was packed, not by hockey fans, but by those who wanted a look at the seven players who claimed they'd seen the monster. There was a television crew from Japan filming the game, and another one from Mexico. There were reporters and tourists and even a crazy man with a rainbow fright wig holding up a sign saying that "The End of the World Has Come," complete with a crude drawing of a dinosaur – not even an Albertosaurus – to back up his claim.

Nish, apparently, had even signed some autographs. But if Nish liked all the attention, Travis hated it. He was captain of the Screech Owls, and the Screech Owls were in tatters. Their lineup was as confused as a game of pick-up-sticks. They didn't seem to have a coach. They had played the worst game of their lives against the Werewolves. And considering they had come out to Alberta to work on their "focus," they were so out of focus as they headed onto the ice to face the Predators that some of the Owls had even forgotten what position Kelly Block had decided they now played.

"I think I'm a goalie," Jeremy joked. "The pads have my name on them, anyway."

Jeremy wasn't even set to start this critical

game. Block wanted to go with his Unit: Jenny in net, Sarah and Jesse on defence, and Lars, Andy, and Travis up front. All of them at positions they had never before played.

"Let this experience bring us together," Kelly Block had told them in the dressing room. "Let us use the crowd for energy. Let us show the world that the Screech Owls stand for the truth, not lies!"

"What the heck did that mean?" Nish hissed to Travis as the Owls made their way down the corridor towards the ice surface.

"I haven't got a clue," said Travis. "Maybe he saw the Albertosaurus, too."

"Mental Block seems awfully upbeat for a guy who's about to embarrass himself in front of a full rink."

"Yeah, I know. He's weird, that's for sure."

Up ahead, Sarah turned around abruptly.

"You guys see Data?"

Travis said nothing. He knew Data hadn't been on the bus. He knew Data was staying deliberately back at the camp, pretending to be "tired." In fact, Data had told Travis he wanted to check around when no one else was there. For what, Travis didn't know. Probably Data didn't know, either. But Travis was still all for Data looking.

"Data's got too many brains to associate himself with this disaster," said Nish.

"You're probably right," said Travis.

There was no more talking to be done. They were at the rink boards now, the noise of the crowd so loud they couldn't hear each other. The crowd was not, however, cheering for hockey. They were cheering for celebrity. The Screech Owls were now world-famous. They had made CNN. They were on the supermarket tabloids.

They were the kids who had seen the dinosaur!

Just to be sure, Data had checked everywhere. He had rolled himself up the ramp into the kitchen and looked for signs of life – even a repairman or a cleaner. But there was no one. The cook must have gone to town for groceries. The Camp Victory parking lot was empty of vehicles. The Owls' bus was at the rink. Kelly Block's fancy 4x4 truck was missing. There was just Data – all alone.

He had told Mr. Dillinger he didn't feel well, but he'd known immediately that Mr. Dillinger wasn't buying it. Mr. Dillinger didn't argue with him, though. Data could tell by the look in Mr. Dillinger's eyes that he was as upset as any of the players. This had turned into a hideous, awful experience. If Mr. Dillinger could have, he would have stayed back at the camp with Data and let Kelly Block have exactly what he wanted: total control of the team, the spotlight his alone.

Data had grown deeply suspicious of Kelly Block. Block had ignored him and treated him like some sort of hanger-on, rather than as a real assistant coach, as Muck always treated him. Data seemed to be just a nuisance to Block, always in the way, so now he was out of the way. But he had no intention of lying in his room sulking.

Because he had been largely ignored by Block, Data had found he could pretty much come and go as he wished. He had puzzled over the "psychological profiles" that Kelly Block had been so keen on. He had wondered about the "focus" sessions and the "envisioning" and "imaging" and whatever else was supposedly going on in the minds of his teammates as they struggled to remain the team that Muck Munro had so carefully built over the years.

When Block had met with the six key players, the Unit, Data had tried to listen in by pulling his wheelchair right up to the door and putting his ear to the keyhole. But the drone of Kelly Block's voice had been so low, Data couldn't hear anything clearly and was no wiser about what Block was up to.

He was almost certain, however, that none of the six players in that room had said a word back – and that just didn't seem right.

From the kitchen area, Data made his way around to the office. He tried the door to Kelly Block's inner office and found it locked. He pulled and rattled, but it would not give.

Data had no idea whether it would work, but he had seen a hundred television shows where an actor had sneaked into a locked room by sliding a credit card past the bolt of a locked door and turning the handle. He didn't have a credit card, but he did have his student card, and it was wrapped in plastic hard enough that it felt like a credit card. If the lock was a deadbolt, though, he wouldn't have a chance.

Carefully, Data slipped the card in between the door frame and the lock. He worked it down, then up, then down again, and felt it rest against something hard.

He pushed, pushed again, and felt something give way. He pushed again, harder, and turned the handle at the same time.

He was in!

"We've got to do *something*!"

Travis heard the anxiety in Sarah's voice, but could not even look up to see her expression. He was beat, exhausted. His heart was pounding wildly and his breathing felt as if someone had stuffed his lungs with cotton balls, leaving no room for oxygen.

He kept his head down, the sweat dripping off his forehead and into his eyes. He flipped up the mask, plucked the towel from around his neck – thank heavens Mr. Dillinger was still here! – and wiped his face.

When he finally looked up, Sarah was still

staring at him, challenging. "Travis!" she said. "*It's up to us!*"

Travis nodded. He knew. The Predators had moved immediately in front when Fahd, on for the power play, had tried to get a little too fancy in his own end and attempted to beat the fore-check. He'd lost the puck – "It stuck in a wet spot!" Fahd claimed, near tears – and the checker had been left alone with Jenny in goal, who got a piece of his sharp shot but had the puck dribble down her back and in when she flopped back in desperation.

The Owls were going nowhere. They couldn't mount a breakout, they couldn't hang on to the puck in the Predators' end, they couldn't send the quick skaters, like Dmitri, off on fast breaks, because, of course, skaters like Dmitri and Sarah were now playing defence.

All they could do was try to hold the Predators at bay. So long as they played one-on-one check-ing hockey – sticking close to their opposite numbers on the Prince Albert team – they could just manage to stay in the game. Sarah, of course, was probably the finest checking centre Travis had ever seen at peewee level. Now, on defence, she seemed uncertain where she should be, but she never left her check.

Early in the second period, the Predators went ahead by a second goal when Nish, playing centre, tried to hit Wilson breaking up left wing but had his pass knocked out of the air by a pinching Predator defender. The Predator threw a cross-ice pass to a teammate just circling behind Jenny, and the teammate tipped the puck in the far side.

Predators 2, Owls 0.

"*Chemistry!*" Kelly Block kept yelling. "*Chemistry!*"

"Biology!" Nish mumbled back. "History! Math! Recess!"

Travis was giggling on the bench when Block suddenly leaned low over his shoulder and, for once, said something that made sense.

"I'm going to try moving Sarah up front," he said. "I want you to switch over to left, and I'll try Dmitri on right."

What a phony! Travis thought. Here's this guy pretending he's just come up with his own new line combination. *But all he was doing was putting back the original first line – Muck's line!*

"*Let's do it!*" Sarah shouted as she leapt over the boards with new energy.

"*Yes!*" shouted Dmitri, who hardly ever shouted anything.

For Travis, it was like putting on his old sneakers after a painful Sunday morning in church shoes. From the moment they lined up for the faceoff, he felt as if he had found his game again. Sarah waiting for the puck to drop, her skates stuttering back and forth. Dmitri with his stick blade flat on the ice, poised to break. And back on defence, Nish, the former centre.

Sarah took the puck before it could even strike the ice. The linesman jumped back and Sarah used him as a shield while she circled quickly, throwing off the Predators' centre. She fired the puck hard off the left boards.

Travis knew his play. He was back in his own world now. As soon as he saw Sarah look at the boards, he took off, bolting around the Predators' defender at the blueline and picking the puck up as it bounced off the boards on the other side of the flailing player.

He had it on his stick now – puck, stick, hands, arms, body, legs, skates, all in familiar territory for the first time in two games. He didn't even need to look to know what Dmitri would be doing.

Flipping the puck high, Travis lobbed it past the outstretched glove hand of the remaining defence. The Predators' player was wisely trying to stay between Travis and Dmitri to block the shot, but when Travis flipped the puck the defender fell for the bait and tried to knock it out of the air. To do so required stopping, and stopping ended his backward progress. Dmitri was already past him, the puck slapping onto the ice and into the embrace of his stick blade.

Dmitri was in alone, and Travis already knew exactly what would happen. The shoulder fake, the move to the backhand, the goalie going down to protect the post, the puck flying high and hard over the goaltender's shoulder, the water bottle flying.

Predators 2, Owls 1.

Data stared at the bookcase, his mind racing.

Kelly Block must have had a thousand books in his office. Most were on psychology and sports psychology and motivation, but here was an entire bookcase devoted to a single, unexpected topic.

Hypnosis!

Data scanned the titles. *Stage Hypnotism: Mass Illusion. Hypnosis and the Control of Fantasy. You Can Control the Minds of Others. Triggering Minds. The Art of Suggestive Hypnotism.* . . .

And on the bottom shelf there were at least a dozen videos, all devoted to the art of hypnotism. There was hypnotism for psychologists, hypnotism for therapists, even hypnotism for circus performers.

Data moved to the filing cabinet. He knew what he was doing was wrong, but he was starting to believe that whatever Kelly Block had been doing was even more wrong. He didn't like snooping – but he liked even less what had been happening to his friends. And if the only way to correct a terrible wrong was to do something just slightly wrong, and which hurt no one, then Data felt, on balance, he would be right.

The filing cabinet was locked. He tried the desk drawers. Nothing. He tried the pen drawer. Nothing. He picked a small wooden box off the desk and rattled it. There were keys inside.

Data had difficulty manoeuvring. His right arm was almost as good as new but he still couldn't do much with the other one. It took him more than ten minutes, but he finally found the right key and got the drawer open. He had to reach up and grab files at random, lifting them high enough to read what they were.

"CORRESPONDENCE"

"GUARANTEES."

"REPAIR WORK, COMPLETED."

"REPAIR WORK, SCHEDULED."

He was getting nowhere fast. He selected a lower drawer.

He could see these files. His eyes moved quickly, trying to take everything in at once.

"RESERVATIONS."

He pulled the file out and glanced quickly at the record. The Owls were the only team to come to Camp Victory so far this year. That explained the musty smell they had detected when they first arrived. It was only March, however.

But there were hardly any bookings for the months to come. A couple in June, three in July, then more blank spaces.

Data looked at the previous year's bookings. More blank spaces.

He put the file back and searched for another that had caught his eye. "FINANCIAL STATEMENT."

He pulled out the file and opened it. Why hadn't he paid more attention in business class? The statement, stamped by a local accounting firm, made very little sense, but Data knew just enough to come to a quick conclusion.

Camp Victory was losing money – big time.

He selected another file. "BANKS."

The letters enclosed were far more easy to interpret. Some were registered letters. Some read like legal documents. Camp Victory was on the verge of being declared bankrupt. Kelly Block had been given huge loans – hundreds of thousands of dollars – and the banks wanted their money back.

Data was about to close the drawer when a file he hadn't noticed caught his attention.

"CAMP DINOSAUR BUSINESS PLAN."

He plucked the file out, placed it on his lap, and opened it.

"This is a business plan for a new Alberta tourist enterprise to be known as Camp Dinosaur," the opening paragraph began. "It is based on an anticipated surge in international tourism, attracted to the most renowned dinosaur grounds in the world: the Drumheller Badlands. Camp Dinosaur, with an initial start-up investment of $5 million, will capitalize on increased interest in the Badlands and the Royal Tyrrell Museum, and will feature expeditions into the dinosaur grounds in search of fossils and prehistoric evidence. The Jurassic Park theory of the possibility of restoring dinosaur life will be a central theme to this ambitious and easily realized project. An initial share offering of . . ."

Data had seen enough.

Now he knew.

In the third period, Kelly Block began throwing Travis's line out on every second shift, his "chemistry" theories forgotten, as most of the team were back in their original positions. They were almost the Screech Owls again. All they needed now was Muck Munro behind the bench and Kelly Block out of their lives and, just as importantly, out of their minds.

Fahd, of all people, scored the equalizer when he picked up a loose puck in the opposition's end after Derek had squeezed a Predator out of the play. Fahd had meant to pass over to Wilson, pinching in off the far defence, but the puck had glanced the wrong way off Fahd's stick, catching everyone, especially the Predators' goaltender, off guard. With the goalie committed, all she could do was look back helplessly as she slid out towards Wilson, and the puck drifted in over the line.

"We're going to have to do it," Sarah said as the seconds ticked down.

Travis nodded. He knew their line would be on in the final moments.

They changed on the fly, Kelly Block worried now that he'd never get the whistle he was hoping for in the Predators' end. Sarah hit the ice first, racing back into her own end as Nish circled behind the Screech Owls' net with the puck. Nish saw Sarah coming, and dropped the puck for her. He then "pic-ed" the first incoming checker to give Sarah free space up the side.

Travis leapt for the ice as Simon lunged to get off. He hit the ice in full motion, and flew cross-ice, Sarah hitting him with a perfect pass just onside, and Travis cut for the Predators' blueline.

He used the boards to get clear of the first check, but the defence had him lined up perfectly, so he stopped hard and circled. Sarah was flying over centre, with Dmitri now on the ice and charging down his off wing. Travis faked the pass, losing one of the defenders.

Nish was coming late. Travis just dropped the puck so it was on side, barely inside the Predators' blueline, and skated hard for the remaining defender, forcing him to shift sideways in the hopes of beating Nish to the puck. But Nish was already there.

Nish picked up the drop pass in full flight. He had a clear route to the net, the Predators' goaltender skittering out to cut off the angle.

Nish raised his stick for the hard slapper.

The goalie went down on his pads, glove ready.

Nish dropped his stick, and danced sideways, skirting the helpless goaltender and lofting the puck easily into the wide-open net.

Screech Owls 3, Predators 2.

Data was sweating. He knew he would need the files as evidence, particularly the business plan that revealed that Camp Victory was about to be transformed into a dinosaur adventure camp where tourists would scour the Badlands in search of fossils – perhaps even hoping to find proof that dinosaurs hadn't all died out a hundred million years ago. He had the business-plan file, and the bank file, and the reservations file. He would need them all.

He was worried sick he'd be caught. This was break and enter. This was stealing.

But what about Kelly Block? Data still wasn't sure what he had been up to, but he knew, in his heart, that Block had done something to his friends. Something wrong. And he knew that Block was behind this whole mad rush to Drumheller to see if there really was a live dinosaur hiding out among the Badlands.

He wheeled outside and carefully shut the door, listening to the lock click back in place.

He turned, the files on his lap, and began steering his chair out towards the front door. He would go to his cabin, he figured, and there he would hide the files.

Just as Data was about to reach the door he heard a sound outside.

He stopped so hard the files spilled to the floor. He scrambled to pick them up, leaning far out of his wheelchair to reach the papers that had slid across the polished hardwood.

It was a car door slamming!

Data's heart was pounding. He had the last of the files gathered up, but nowhere to hide them or, for that matter, himself. He would have to bluff his way past whoever had just pulled into the parking area.

He opened the door, cringing. Better to be seen leaving the office than to be caught inside, he figured. The sun cut into his eyes. He squinted in the light, unable to see anything but the blinding red and yellow through his eyelids.

"Data?" a voice called.

He recognized that voice. But it couldn't be . . .

Data closed his eyes hard, then slowly opened them.

A man was paying off a cab driver. The cabby was pulling away. And then the man was standing in the centre of the parking lot, smiling, an old suitcase in one hand, his other hand raised in greeting.

"MUCK!" Data called. His voice broke. He had never been so glad to see anyone in his life.

Travis was passing along the handshake line, Nish behind him, Sarah in front. He was tapping shin pads and punching gloves, and trying to say the right thing – "Nice game . . . Thanks for the game. . . . Good game" – but he knew it should never have been this close. The Owls had been lucky to get the win in the end, but they should have beaten the Predators easily. And they should never have lost to the Werewolves.

Without even looking at the standings posted in the lobby, the Owls all knew where this left them. The win had given them one more game in the tournament, but not for the championship. They had made it to the "B" side, and would play for the consolation title. It wasn't the same as making the big game.

In a way, though, it hardly mattered. For the first time ever, the Owls would probably have preferred just to go home and not play at all any more. The excitement had all been off the ice instead of on. Drumheller was a wonderful town, but Kelly Block had made their stay an experience they would rather forget. And as long as he was around, none of them felt much like playing. He wasn't their coach – and they weren't the old Screech Owls.

Sarah waited until Travis had passed the last Predator in the line, then together they turned towards the exit.

"Do you see what I see?" she asked.

"What?"

"What?" repeated Nish from behind.

"By the Zamboni entrance."

The doors were open, the big machine ready to come out and flood the ice after the handshakes were over. But to one side was Data, pumping his fist in the air.

And behind Data, holding on to the handles of his wheelchair, was Muck!

13

"WE OWE YOU YOUNG PEOPLE AN APOLOGY."

The deep and confident voice belonged to the senior officer in the Drumheller detachment of the Royal Canadian Mounted Police. He was standing in the centre of the camp kitchen, the only room large enough to hold all those who had been called together for this moment.

Travis sat at a table with the other six who had seen the dinosaur. Nish was beaming, as if he were about to be knighted by the inspector. Sarah was there, smiling. And Lars, Andy, Jesse, Jenny. All of them. And all of their teammates. And, of course, Muck.

"Mr. Block has been arraigned this morning in a Calgary court. He is in custody, pending Monday's bail hearing. We cannot comment on the charges or the case, of course, but we can tell you that it seems you were right and we were wrong to doubt you."

"ALLLLL RIIIIGHT!" Nish shouted. Everyone in the room, Mounties and players, looked at him as if he had just dropped in from another planet.

"We knew, naturally, that there never was any dinosaur," said the inspector. "That was impossible. But we knew nothing about the powers of hypnotism and suggestion. I'm told, however, that while under hypnosis, you can't be made to do anything you don't *wish* to do, but you can be made to imagine things, even as a group, if conditions are right and the hypnotist knows what he is doing."

It was all becoming clear to Travis. Nish, after all, had said he'd fallen asleep while undergoing that one-on-one session with Block, and they'd thought it a great joke, but it now seemed clear that Nish was *intended* to fall asleep. All the other talk, about "chemistry" and "focus," was just blarney while Block used the hot room and his purring voice to get people to fall under his hypnotic spell. And the fan that Travis had watched before he dozed off – it was the same thing. All part of the scheme.

"You will be interested to know that my men did indeed find something in exactly the place you identified out in the hills," the inspector continued.

Travis could sense the room go very quiet.

The inspector laughed. "No, I'm afraid *not* an Albertosaurus, though I think some of my officers wondered at times if they might come face to face with a monster."

Everyone chuckled politely. Travis and Nish strained to see what it was that two of the Mounties were carrying into the room.

"This," the inspector continued, "is a remote-control sound system. It's not very big, you'll notice. But it certainly sounds big."

One of the officers flipped a switch. The machine hissed, then growled deeply, the fierce sound filling the room and threatening to burst the walls.

The roar of the Albertosaurus!

"Turn it down, Mac!" the inspector shouted. The machine clicked off. "We believe this device was hidden out there by someone, probably our Mr. Block. It was set off by a remote sensor. Body movement, say a bike passing by, would set it off. Anything that happened after that probably took place in your imaginations."

In some ways it was really quite simple, thought Travis. Block had probably found it quite easy to insert the idea of a living Albertosaurus in their heads. They'd all seen the life-size models at the Royal Tyrrell Museum and were all excited about dinosaurs. All they had to do was hear that sound, and their minds would do the rest of the work for Block. He'd probably experimented first with Nish, who obviously had the wildest imagination on the team, and then tried it out on the six he'd selected.

They weren't a Russian unit at all. And their selection had nothing whatsoever to do with playing hockey.

It had everything to do with a very public hoax, and millions of dollars.

"I think Mr. Munro has something to say to you all," the inspector said.

He nodded to Muck, who fidgeted awkwardly, then stepped forward. Nish began a small smattering of applause that caught on, and grew. Muck grimaced and shut them down by raising his right hand.

"We have a game to play," Muck announced. "We're still here for a hockey tournament."

14

THE DRUMHELLER RINK WAS FILLED TO CAPACITY for the second straight day – but the crowd was hardly the same this time. This time the merely curious had stayed at home. The people of Drumheller had come out to see hockey, not the little kids who had played a part in what the papers were now calling the "hoax of the century."

The crowd had gathered early. The big championship game was still two hours off, but they had come to cheer for the Screech Owls, and also to show them that in Drumheller they were not all like Kelly Block. They cheered the warmup and they clapped for the players coming onto the ice and they even cheered when Travis Lindsay, the little captain, succeeded in firing a puck off the crossbar and over the glass into the crowd.

The Owls were up against the Lethbridge Lasers, a fine team that had missed the championship round by a single goal. Since the Owls had struggled so badly, even against weak teams, the crowd expected the Lasers would have little trouble taking the consolation title.

Muck's entire speech before the game, Travis figured, could be written down on a tiny scrap of paper and stuffed inside a fortune cookie.

"Same lines as always," he said. "Jeremy and Jenny split the goaltending. Play your best."

Nothing about "chemistry," no fancy words out of a psychology textbook, no crazy theories – and certainly no hypnotism.

Sarah and Travis and Dmitri started.

They dominated the first shift, up and down the ice, with pinpoint passing and deft drop plays that sent Dmitri in for a superb chance, only to be turned back by a fine stacked-pads save by the Lasers' goalie.

Halfway through the first period, Nish saw little Simon Milliken breaking for centre and threw a high pass that went over Simon's shoulder like a football and dropped just ahead of him a second before he crossed centre ice. Simon was onside and had a clear break. He went backhand-forehand and then slipped the puck in on the short side as the goalie butterflied too late.

Screech Owls 1, Lasers 0.

It was clear there was not going to be much scoring. First Jenny and then Jeremy, who came in at the halfway point, played magnificently. The Lasers' goaltender, staying in for the whole game, seemed unbeatable except for Simon's lucky break.

Into the third period the Lasers finally struck when they turned a two-on-one into an open chance. Wilson, backpedalling fast, guessed it would be a pass and dropped to block it, but the Laser centre held fast to the puck and slipped it quickly across in front of Jeremy, and the winger fired it fast into the open side.

Owls 1, Lasers 1.

What a game it had become. The crowd was screaming with every rush. If this was a consolation match, Travis thought, what would the championship game be like?

Travis watched happily as Muck walked along behind the players the way he had a thousand times before. Mr. Dillinger was back, patting backs, rapping helmets, dropping towels around necks, slapping pants as players rose and leapt over the boards and into the play. Ty was once again Ty, whispering strategy to Muck and talking to the players about other things they might try, and complimenting them on the things they were doing right.

If I could spend the rest of my life on this team, Travis thought, *I would*. And then he realized what that meant.

Chemistry.

The Screech Owls had had it all along. It took Kelly Block to ruin it.

The consolation match ended in a tie, 1–1, and they announced an immediate ten-minute, sudden-death overtime. First goal wins.

Muck was at Travis's back, leaning down.

"Don't be afraid to carry," Muck said. "They're keying on Sarah and Nish, expecting them to have the puck."

Travis nodded. He felt Muck's big, rough hand on his neck. It was like a comforter.

Next shift, Wilson pounded the puck around the boards to Nish, who stopped, seeming almost to tread water as he stared down the ice, challenging the Lasers to forecheck.

Travis turned back sharply, rapping his stick on the blueline as he cut into his own end. Nish hit him perfectly.

A winger was chasing him, closing in on him fast. Without thinking, Travis did something he had only dreamed about before. Still skating towards his own net with the puck, he suddenly dropped it back so it passed through the checker's skates. At the same time, Travis turned abruptly, picking up his own back pass as he headed straight up ice towards the Laser end.

He could hear the roar of the crowd. What sound would they have made, he wondered, if it hadn't worked?

The roar of the Albertosaurus?

Travis moved over the red line, with Sarah ahead of him, slowing so she wouldn't go offside.

The Lasers were double-teaming her. Travis bent as if to fire a pass in her direction, then brought the heel of his stick down hard on the puck – sending it backwards through his own skates!

Travis cringed, praying that Dmitri would be there.

He was!

Dmitri had read the play perfectly. He took up the sliding puck and flew across the line, Sarah and Travis barely staying onside, each with one leg straddling the Lasers' blueline.

Dmitri broke for the corner, spinning away.

Travis read the signal. Dmitri was going to drop the puck and take out his checker. They were cycling the puck – Russian style.

Travis headed for the corner, and the puck came instantly back to him. Dmitri had the checker under control – he'd have to be careful he didn't get called for interference – and Travis looked back towards the blueline, certain of what he would see there.

A locomotive coming full bore: Wayne Nishikawa.

Nish was already poised to shoot, his stick sweeping back for the one-timer.

Travis held to the last microsecond, then sent the puck out fast. Nish had to time it perfectly. He brought his stick down hard.

The puck shot forward, then Travis lost it, then the crowd roared as one.

Travis spun, looking at the net. It was bulging with the puck. The Lasers' goalie was fully extended, legs out, arms out, stick swinging wildly – but the puck was already by him.

We did it! Travis shouted.

The Owls poured onto the ice. Travis heard Sarah screaming in his ear.

"Trav! We won! WE WON!"

It looked as if the Screech Owls had won the Stanley Cup, not the consolation round of a small-town tournament. The entire arena seemed to explode, as if all that had happened to the Owls was now forgotten, as if everything in the world was now right once more and would never go wrong again.

Ty was running into the crowd of Screech Owls that had smothered Nish into a corner.

Even Muck was out on the ice, moving as fast as his bad leg would take him. He was holding both arms in the air, fists up high, a big grin from ear to ear. Behind Muck, Mr. Dillinger was pushing Data out onto the ice, Data's fist pumping the air.

Travis and Sarah pushed into the crowd. Dmitri leaned over and smacked Travis's helmet. It rattled his brain but felt like a caress. Travis threw his arm around Sarah's shoulder and hugged. Jenny leaped onto their backs from behind.

They threw their gloves and sticks and helmets off, and pushed and shoved and cheered and screamed until, finally, they broke through to reach the Screech Owl who had scored the winning goal in overtime.

Nish was beet-red and covered in sweat, but there was no smile on his face, no life in his eyes. "What's going on?" he asked Travis. "What's everybody yelling about?"

"You, you stupid idiot – great goal! WONDER-FUL GOAL!"

"*What goal?*"

"We won, you jerk. Don't you realize what you've done."

Nish shook his head, not comprehending. "I can't remember a thing," he said.

"*What?*" Travis yelled, unbelieving.

"I must have been hypnotized."

And then Nish winked.

THE END

The Ghost of the Stanley Cup

The Screech Owls have come to Ottawa to play at the magnificent Corel Centre in the Little Stanley Cup Pee Wee Tournament. It is the trip of a lifetime: part hockey, part sightseeing, part adventure – part terror.

This relaxed summer event honours Lord Stanley himself – the Canadian Governor General who donated the Stanley Cup – and gives young hockey players a chance to see the wonders of Canada's capital city, travel into the wilds of Algonquin Park – and even go river rafting.

Yet everywhere the Owls go, it seems they are bumping into spooks, including the ghost of the famous painter Tom Thomson.

Why have these phantoms come back? And why are they trying to reach the Screech Owls? . . . And why now, when the Owls were looking good to make it to the tournament final?

Chapter 1

NISH WAS DEAD!

One moment he was screaming "*I'M GONNA HURL!*" from the seat behind Travis Lindsay – who was desperately hanging on to the bucking, slamming, sliding monster beneath them – the next he was airborne, a chubby twelve-year-old in a red crash helmet, a black rubber wetsuit, and a yellow life jacket, spinning high over the rest of the Screech Owls and smack into the churning whirlpool at the bottom of the most dangerous chute of the long rapids.

Nish entered his watery grave without a sound, the splash instantly erased by the rushing, tea-coloured water of the mighty Ottawa River as it choked itself through the narrow canyon of wet, dripping rock and roared triumphantly out the other end. Screaming and spinning one second, he was gone the next – his teammates so terrified they could do nothing but tighten their iron-locked grips on their paddles and the rope of the river raft.

Nish was dead!

Travis closed his eyes to the slap of cold water as it cuffed off the dripping rock walls and spilled in over his face. *Would any of them get out alive? Would it be up to him, as team captain and best friend, to tell Nish's mother?*

"Did my little Wayne have any last words?" poor sweet Mrs. Nishikawa would ask.

"Yes," Travis would have to answer.

"What were they?" Mrs. Nishikawa would say, a Kleenex held to her trusting eyes.

And Travis would have to tell her: "*'I'm gonna hurl.'*"

The Screech Owls had come to Ottawa for a special edition of the Little Stanley Cup. Instead of in January or February, it was being held over the Canada Day long weekend and was going to honour the one hundredth anniversary of the Ottawa Silver Seven – hockey's very first Stanley Cup dynasty. It was to be a peewee hockey tournament the likes of which had never been seen before. The Hockey Hall of Fame in Toronto was bringing up the original Stanley Cup that Governor General Lord Stanley had given to the people of Canada in 1893, there was going to be a special display of hockey memorabilia from the early 1900s, and the Governor General herself was going to present the cup to the winning team. The Sports Network was going to televise the final, and special rings – "*Stanley Cup rings!*" Nish had shouted when he heard – would be awarded to the champions.

But it was unlike other tournaments for more reasons than that. Muck Munro, who always said he had little use for summer hockey, wasn't there to coach. Muck had told them he couldn't get off work, but the Owls figured he hadn't tried all that hard. If Muck took a summer holiday, he preferred to head into the bush for a week of trout fishing. Muck's two assistants, Barry and Ty, hadn't been able to get away either. The team was essentially under the control of good old Mr. Dillinger, who was wonderful at sharpening skates but didn't know much about breakout patterns, and Larry Ulmar – Data – who was great at cheering but not much for strategy. Right now, Data was waiting for the Owls at the end of the ride, deeply disappointed that the river guides hadn't been able to figure out a way to strap his wheelchair into the big, bucking rafts.

Nor were the Screech Owls staying with local families for this tournament. Instead, they were camping, along with most of the other teams, at a church camp farther down the river, within sight of the highrises of Ottawa. It was an ideal location, and the tournament games were deliberately spaced out to allow for day trips. The teams were booked to go river rafting, mountain biking in the Gatineau Hills, and even off to world-famous Algonquin Park, where they hoped to see moose and bear. The tournament final itself was to be played in the Corel Centre, where the Ottawa Senators had played only the winter before. Nish had said it was only proper that he win his first Stanley Cup ring on a rink where NHL stars had skated.

But now Nish was lost overboard, bouncing, spinning, bumping along the bottom of the Ottawa River, snapping turtles pulling at his desperately clutching fingers, leeches already sucking out his blood.

It had been the guide's suggestion that one of them join him at the back of the raft and help steer. Nish, of course, had jumped up first with both hands raised and shouted out that the seat was his. The new player, Samantha Bennett, had also raised her hand to volunteer, and Travis was quick to notice a small flash of anger in Sam's green eyes when the guide gave in and picked Nish. Sam, who'd only moved to Tamarack two months earlier, was Data's replacement on defence. Big and strong, she was as competitive off the ice as on, and almost as loud and just possibly as funny as Nish himself. Andy Higgins had even started calling her "Nish-*ette*," though never to her face. Nish, to her, was a rival as top Screech Owls' defender, not an example for her to copy.

The waters had been calm when Nish went back to sit with the guide. Once, Travis thought he had seen Nish unbuckle his safety harness while the real guide — "Call me Hughie" — pointed out the sights along the river. Travis hadn't worried about Nish's harness until, around the next bend in the river, his ears were filled with a frightening roar, and the water, now rushing, loomed white and foaming ahead of them.

It hadn't seemed possible to Travis that a rubber raft could chance such a run. What if it was punctured on the rocks? But the guide had sent them straight into the highest boils of the current, and the huge raft had folded and sprung and tossed several of them out of their seats as it slid and jumped and smashed through the water. They turned abruptly at the bottom and rammed head-on into a rooster tail of rolling water, the rush now flinging them backwards as if shot from a catapult.

Nish had held on fine through all that – despite his undone safety harness.

Down the river they went, the water roaring and thundering between tight rocks as the runs grew more and more intense. But always the big raft came through, the Screech Owls screaming happily and catching their breath each time they made it down a fast run and shot out the other side into calmer, deeper waters.

But this last time had been too much. The big raft slid into the channel, snaking over the rises, and up ahead Nish saw Lars Johanssen, Wilson Kelly, and Sarah Cuthbertson being bounced right out of their seats. But they had their hands looped carefully around the rope, as instructed, and fortunately they came right back down.

Travis had also left his seat, the quick feeling of weightlessness both exhilarating and alarming. He held tight and bounced back down, hard, and was instantly into the next rise.

That was when he heard his great friend's famous last words – *"I'M GONNA HURL!"* – and the next moment he was watching, helpless, as Nish slipped into that horrifying watery grave.

Nish, lost overboard.

Drowned.

His body never to be recovered.

THE SCREECH OWLS SERIES

EW!

E SCREECH OWLS
RAPBOOK

OY MacGREGOR

with fun, trivia, stats, and background information
most famous peewee hockey team in the world!

ing you always wanted to know about the Screech Owls
, Muck, Mr. Dillinger, and highlights from the team's
dventures.

ted in full colour by Screech Owls artist Greg Banning.
le now at bookstores everywhere.